Praise for Ally Blue's *Adder*

"Right from the start I absolutely loved the voice of this novel. I felt like I was traveling in the underworld of grunge/alternate music."

Cascade, Two Lips Reviews

"...a phenomenal story with larger than life characters who ensnare the reader from the start."

Teresa, Rainbow Reviews

Look for these titles by
Ally Blue

Now Available:

Bay City Paranormal Investigations Series:
Oleander House (Book 1)
What Hides Inside (Book 2)
Twilight (Book 3)
Closer (Book 4)
An Inner Darkness (Book 5)
Love, Like Ghosts (Book 6)

Print Anthologies:
Hearts from The Ashes
Temperature's Rising

Willow Bend
Love's Evolution
Eros Rising
Catching a Buzz
Fireflies
Untamed Heart
The Happy Onion
Where the Heart Is
Dragon's Kiss

Adder

Ally Blue

A Samhain Publishing, Ltd. publication.

Samhain Publishing, Ltd.
577 Mulberry Street, Suite 1520
Macon, GA 31201
www.samhainpublishing.com

Adder

Print ISBN: 978-1-60504-541-2
Digital ISBN: 978-1-60504-487-3

Editing by Sasha Knight
Cover by Anne Cain

First Samhain Publishing, Ltd. electronic publication: April 2009
First Samhain Publishing, Ltd. print publication: February 2010

Dedication

To my family, for their unwavering support. I love you all! And as always, to the best critique group in the world, for sticking with me through yet another book and lending their unique insight. I've said it before and I'll say it again: I'd never get anything written without them.

Special thanks to Jet's SO, for his help with some particulars of the music biz. You are a doll! As to those details, any mistakes you see are solely mine.

Chapter One

Adder's first punch broke Bull's nose.

"Son of a bitch!" Bull roared. Dropping his drumsticks, he tackled Adder to the stage and the brawl was on.

By the time security pulled them apart, Adder had a black eye, a sprained wrist and Bull's blood smeared all over him, but he didn't care. It felt too fucking good to finally knock that smug look off Bull's too-handsome-to-be-real face.

It *used* to be handsome, anyway. At the moment it looked more like a couple miles of bad road.

Adder grinned, tonguing the gap where Bull had knocked out one of his teeth. Maybe he should get a gold tooth. He could afford it now.

Swooping down to grab his abandoned mic while Bull shook off the security guards and staggered offstage, Adder faced the pack of glitter-and-rags-clad teenagers milling at his feet. "Ladies and gentlemen, we appear to be short one drummer at this time." He glanced sideways. Said drummer had apparently passed out on the floor.

Sadly, the cause was more likely the coke he'd snorted earlier than Adder's fists. Stupid micro-brained jock bastard. If he was dim enough to keep breaking Adder's one and only rule—never allow recreational substances to interfere with your performance—he deserved what he got. Nothing fucked up a perfectly good show quite like a drummer who couldn't keep time.

"For the record," Adder said, pointing an accusing finger at Bull, "the Neanderthal there is fired. Somebody tell him that when he wakes up."

The audience went wild. Adder laughed. It amused him how much his fans loved his temper tantrums. The inevitable drama seemed to draw as many people to his shows as the music did. More, maybe.

That was fine with him. Adder held no illusions regarding the reasons for the sudden popularity which had hit during this, his twenty-second summer. He played a dozen different instruments, he wrote brilliant songs and possessed a rich, agile baritone, but people didn't fall at his feet because of his talent. No, his increasing hordes of fans adored him because he was beautiful, intimidating, infuriating and altogether larger than life. He knew this, and saw no point in pretending otherwise.

After years of hard work and single-minded purpose, he was finally on the brink of the stardom he'd been chasing since he left home at fifteen. How he got there was, in his considered opinion, immaterial.

Tossing a hank of sweat-soaked green hair out of his eyes, he favored his audience with a dazzling—if slightly bloody and gap-toothed—smile. "Well now. Where were we, before my former percussionist fucked everything up?" He pretended to think it over, ignoring the song requests, declarations of undying love and various lewd propositions being shouted at him. "Oh yes. We were about to play 'Pixie Dust' for you."

The crowd screamed like a many-headed ravening monster. Adder laughed as he snatched his violin from its stand. Playing that song was going to be a bitch with a sprained wrist, but he'd be damned if he'd let that stop him. There were only two songs left in the set. The swooping high of performing, coupled with the adoration of his fans, would carry him through the pain. Then after the show, he'd pick one lucky girl or boy from the audience to help him feel better.

Maybe one of each, he amended, winking at the young man and woman holding hands in the front row and practically drooling on his silver ankle boots. They looked like they might actually be legal, thank all the gods. Adder would cheerfully admit to being a slut, but he refused to fuck—or be fucked by—anyone under eighteen. Being branded as a sex offender wouldn't do anything good for his career.

All-ages shows were a bitch like that. The next one was eighteen and over only. *Much* easier to find a nice adult fuck in *that* crowd.

Tucking his trusty violin under his chin, he touched the bow to the strings and glanced over at Vi. The keyboardist gave him a nod and a grin. She tapped one purple-painted nail on the drum machine she'd already set up.

Adder snickered. They always seemed to end up with the electronic drummer eventually. Oh well.

"This is for all you pixies out there," he purred into the mic. "One...two...three..."

"The thing is," Harpo mused three and a half weeks and eleven gigs later, sprawled across the rug on the floor of the band's Midtown Atlanta apartment, "we *need* a good drummer. That stupid machine just doesn't cut it."

Shrugging, Adder took a swig from his bottle of Mike's Hard

Lime. He draped one long leg over the arm of the sofa. "Yes, well, we've been needing a *good* drummer ever since Karen left. Bull was shit all along."

Vi giggled into her Sangria. "Bull. Shit. Ha!"

Adder aimed a halfhearted barefoot kick in the general direction of Vi's chair. "Has anyone ever told you you're silly when you're drunk?"

"Yeah, you, asshole." Vi threw a wadded-up napkin at him. "That must be why we broke up. You constantly pointing out my many flaws."

"You broke up because both of you demand absolute fidelity, but neither one of you is capable of it yourself." Harpo sat up, slender fingers fluffing the bleached-blond Afro which had earned him his nickname. "Speaking of which, Adder, you have *got* to stop crawling into bed with me. Sheila about popped an artery last night."

Adder snickered at the memory. The bassist's girlfriend loathed Adder, which meant he couldn't resist pissing her off at every opportunity. "Harpo. Darling. You *know* I have trouble sleeping sometimes. If she can't handle me being in bed with you—in a completely platonic capacity, by the way—you are both perfectly free to stay at her place."

"Fuck you."

"Is that an insult, or an offer?" Adder waggled his brows.

Harpo's cheeks went pink beneath his deep brown complexion. "God, would you stop?"

"Of course. There's no need to call me God."

Vi threw her head back and laughed so hard Adder feared she might break a rib. "Harpo, you know he'd leave you alone if you'd just fuck him already."

With a deep sigh, Harpo pressed the heel of one hand to his

brow. "This conversation is now officially over."

"You brought it up. In a manner of speaking." Adder tucked both legs under him and leaned his elbows on his knees. "Does anyone have ideas on how to find a decent drummer?"

"Advertise?" Vi tucked a strand of her sleek purple pageboy behind one ear and leaned over to set her wineglass on the coffee table. "My friend Jasmine says her band found a singer in three days by putting an ad on craigslist."

"Oh yes, if we want to attract the dregs of drumming society." Adder scratched his bare chest. "We could always recruit someone away from another band. The Unauthorized Penises' drummer is absolutely amazing. I bet she'd defect if I fucked her."

Vi laughed. "Keep dreaming. She's a lesbian."

"*He* is straight, actually." Harpo gave his lip ring a light tug. "You know what, I might know somebody who could help us out."

Adder shot him a skeptical look. "No offense, but I've met some of your friends. They are, to put it kindly, a very strange bunch."

"Says the man who goes through a tube of glitter gel a week and actually wears lederhosen in public." Harpo reached over to swat Adder's bare knee. "Do you want a new drummer or not?"

"All right, I'm listening." Adder slouched against the cushions. "So who's this friend of yours that's such a wonderful drummer?"

"Kalil Sabatino. We went to high school together in Buckhead." Harpo shifted forward to snatch the last of the Hard Lime bottles from the cooler on the coffee table. He twisted the cap off and took a long swallow. "He was a great drummer even then. I saw him at The Tabernacle a couple of weeks ago, playing session for Ozomatli's opener. He's better than ever, and he's looking for a permanent gig."

Intrigued, Adder nodded. "All right. If he's interested, bring him in for an audition."

"When?"

"Tomorrow, if he's available. That way, if he works out we'll have time to get comfortable playing with each other before our next gig."

Vi snorted. Adder shook his head. The girl had such a juvenile sense of humor.

"Done. I'll call him right now." Harpo stood and stretched, showing a hint of fat-free belly when his T-shirt rode up. "Whose turn is it to do dinner? I'm starved."

Adder pointed at Vi, who groaned. "Shit."

"Uh-oh. That means frozen pizza, doesn't it?" Harpo thumped the side of Vi's head on his way to fetch his cell phone from his room. "Put tomatoes on mine."

"I'll give you fucking tomatoes," she grumbled, glaring at Harpo's back.

Adder gave her a curious look. "What does that even mean?"

She turned her gray-eyed glare to Adder. "Shut up."

Laughing, Adder sprang from the sofa and plopped his long, lanky frame down on Vi's rather more petite lap. She let out an annoyed grunt, which Adder ignored. He wound both arms around her and planted a kiss right on her mouth. Without the makeup and purple contacts she wore on stage, she looked young and very girl-next-door, in spite of the violet hair. Ever since their brief fling ended over a year ago, Adder had thought of her almost like a sister. Except for the part where they still fucked now and then.

"I love you, Vi," he murmured, nuzzling her cheek. "Will

you marry me?"

She smacked his thigh just below the hem of his shorts, leaving a red handprint over one coil of his snake tattoo. "Oh sure, it's every girl's dream to get hitched to the biggest manwhore in town."

Grinning, he slid his lips over her jaw to tongue the spot on her throat that always made her shiver. "Fair enough. How about sucking my cock, then?"

"No, I have to make dinner." Giggling now, she attempted—unsuccessfully—to push him off her lap. "Get off me, you horny bastard. Go jerk off like a normal person."

"How is masturbation more normal than real sex?" Sighing, he climbed off Vi's lap. "All right, so I'm rejected once again. I'll be in my room comforting myself."

"Use lube," Vi called as he wandered off. "As often as you abuse your dick, it'll chafe if you don't."

"Sweetheart, feel perfectly free to bite me," he replied without looking back. Behind him, Vi laughed, and Adder grinned.

He passed Harpo in the hallway. "K's meeting us at the studio at three tomorrow," Harpo informed him.

"Wonderful, thank you." Acting on impulse, Adder swooped the smaller man into his arms and pecked him on the lips. "I don't suppose you'd suck my cock? I find myself in need of release."

"For the zillionth time, no, I will not suck your cock, or fuck you, or let you fuck me, or give you a hand job." Harpo extricated himself from Adder's embrace, dark eyes glinting in amusement. "What part of 'I'm straight and not at all interested in your sweaty man-bits' don't you understand?"

"Fine, I understand. Everyone wants me but you and Vi."

"Keeps you on your toes." Harpo smacked Adder's butt before sauntering off toward the living room. "Hey, if you're going in your room to jerk off, stuff a sock in your mouth or something. You're *really* loud."

Adder chuckled as he locked himself in his room and fell onto the bed. The object he stuffed into himself was not a sock, nor was the target orifice his mouth. When he came, he made sure to scream Harpo's name.

Chapter Two

When the cab pulled up in front of the grungy gray metal door, Kalil frowned. "Whoa, hang on, this can't be right."

The cab driver gave him a dirty look. "This is fourteen-oh-four Peachtree Alley. That's where you told me you wanted to go."

"Yeah, but it's supposed to be a recording studio. Or, well, kind of." Kalil gestured at the narrow, dingy alley. "Does this look like a place where someone would put a studio?"

"How the hell do I know? You give me an address, I drive you there, you pay me. I can't help what the fuckin' place looks like."

"I know, but—"

An irritated growl drifted from beneath the driver's ratty blond mustache. "Look, kid, this is the address you gave me, like it or not. So you gettin' out here or what?"

What, Kalil thought, gazing at the unmarked door with extreme trepidation. Was this Harpo's idea of a joke? It was exactly the sort of prank the bastard would've pulled in high school. On the other hand, Kalil had heard about the incident between Adder and Bull, and he knew the band hadn't yet found a new drummer. And if there was one thing you could count on with Harpo, it was how seriously he took his music.

Still trying to convince himself he wasn't about to be mugged—or at least laughed at—Kalil got out of the cab and handed the driver a twenty through the open window. "Keep the change."

"Gee, thanks. Now I can finally have that surgery."

"Jackass," Kalil muttered as the cab peeled away from the curb. He indulged in a moment's nostalgia for his ancient Volkswagen Beetle, which had wheezed its last the previous week, then gathered his courage and approached the dented and rusted door.

He'd knocked three times without answer and was starting to get seriously pissed off at Harpo when the door swung open to reveal a petite, pretty woman with purple hair and a matching minidress. She gave him a dazzling smile. "Oh, you must be Kalil! C'mon in."

She stood aside, and he shuffled past her. "Um. I'm Kalil, yeah. Hi."

"Hi." Grabbing his hand, she shook it hard. "I'm Violet McGill. Vi for short." She shifted her grip to his wrist and pulled him down a cramped, poorly lit and thankfully short hallway. "Sorry it took so long to answer. Harpo and Adder were fucking around and we didn't hear you at first."

Kalil gaped. "They were *what*?" Harpo was an open-minded guy—as evidenced by his schoolboy friendship with Kalil, who'd always been one hundred percent bent—but he was straight. Or at least he *had* been.

Surely things hadn't changed *that* much in the few years since they'd last seen each other.

Vi shot an amused look at him. "They weren't *fucking,* not that Adder hasn't tried. They were fucking *around.* Making weird-ass noises with some of the instruments. They like to do that sort of shit."

"Oh." He grinned, a sudden wave of excitement surging through his blood. He'd agreed to this audition mostly based on his enormous respect for Harpo as a musician, but if this band liked to stretch the boundaries of music as much as he did it could turn out to be a wonderful thing for everyone.

"Here we are," Vi announced as she and Kalil emerged into a large room carpeted in blinding green and yellow shag. "The practice room's through there." She waved at a half-open door in one wall. "This is our lounge area."

"Cool," he lied, trying not to wince. Damn, the place was hideous. Not that it mattered, really, but still. "Where're the guys?"

Before Vi could answer, Harpo's fuzzy blond head popped up from behind the bar in the corner. Grinning, he jumped to his feet and bounded toward Kalil. "Hey hey, Special K!" He grabbed Kalil and hugged him, thumping him on the back so hard it made him cough. "Great to see you again, man, how are you?"

"Fine." Kalil couldn't help returning Harpo's happy smile, in spite of the man's use of the nickname he thought he'd ditched eight years ago. "Thanks for letting me come out and play."

"Harpo recommended you," said a low, melodious voice from somewhere to Kalil's left. "He wouldn't have if you weren't good. I hope you are."

"I am." Turning, Kalil searched for the source of the voice.

The source wasn't hard to spot. Kalil stared open-mouthed at the man leaning against the frame of an open door in the wall beside the bar. He had to be at least a head taller than Kalil, all long sleek limbs and pale skin smudged here and there with dirt and glitter. A gauzy, pale pink shirt dotted with pearl beads hung open on his wide shoulders, framing a sparsely haired chest which gleamed with sweat. The sinuous curve of a bright green snake tattoo wound around his right thigh below the hem of the ragged black shorts. Shaggy shoulder-length hair in a green that matched the tattoo clung in damp clumps to his face and neck. Big hazel eyes regarded Kalil with unabashed interest.

Adder. It had to be. Kalil licked his lips. He'd heard of Adder, of course. Who in the Atlanta music scene hadn't? But damn, he hadn't been prepared for the city's resident oddball singer to be this *hot*.

Kalil drew himself up straight and met Adder's unnervingly direct gaze. "You must be Adder. I'm Kalil Sabatino. It's nice to meet you."

Adder's plump, pouty lips curved into a smile, showing a flash of what appeared to be a stainless-steel tooth. Pushing away from the wall, he padded barefoot across the floor toward Kalil, took his hand and lifted it to his mouth. "Charmed," he breathed, brushing a kiss across the back of Kalil's hand.

Kalil stood there, feeling at once awkward and flattered. He wondered if Adder had this effect on everyone, or if he himself simply possessed a hitherto unsuspected weakness for tall, green-haired men in women's blouses.

Harpo's dark hand closed over Adder's wrist, pulling him away from Kalil and breaking the spell. "Quit flirting." Harpo aimed a fierce frown at Adder, who held up both hands and backed away with an unrepentant grin. Sighing, Harpo turned to face Kalil. "Ignore him. His goal in life is to fuck every living thing on the planet."

"Only humans," Adder protested. "And I don't do jailbait." It wasn't exactly a denial of Harpo's claim.

"Yeah, yeah." Vi emerged from behind the bar with a bottle of water. She took a long swallow. "So, are we gonna play, or what?"

"Play." Harpo clapped Kalil on the shoulder. "You ready? The drum kit's in the practice room. Come on, I'll show you."

Kalil followed Harpo, Adder and Vi through the half-open door into a large room carpeted in soft gray. A surprising variety of instruments took up most of the floor space. The drum set against the back wall was pretty basic, but good enough for an audition. If he landed this position, Kalil could borrow his brother's pickup truck to bring his own kit over.

He nodded. "Looks good. Let's do it."

He strode over and parked himself on the wobbly little throne they'd provided. Drawing his lucky drumsticks from the inner pocket of his denim jacket, he tapped the drums and cymbals a few times, just to get the feel of them. He tried not to notice Adder watching him.

They played "Johnny B. Goode" first, followed by "Bigmouth Strikes Again" and "Take A Walk On The Wild Side". Kalil decided that he should never, ever be within listening distance of Adder when he growled out the latter tune. His sex-soaked delivery made Lou Reed sound innocent, a feat not to be taken lightly. The resulting hard-on was something Kalil could definitely live without while trying to play.

The switch to "Sexy Back" was more than welcome, and not only because Adder's take on the tune leaned to the campy side. Kalil pounded out the staccato rhythm he'd invented to go with his second favorite song, losing himself in the music and thus temporarily forgetting the hypnotic roll of Adder's slender hips against the mic stand.

When Kalil knocked out the final beat on the bass drum, the room went still for a moment. Then Harpo whooped, Vi squealed and Kalil knew he was in. He laughed as two-thirds of his new band rushed up and swept him into an enthusiastic hug.

"Oh my *God,* you're fucking awesome!" Vi pinched his cheeks. "Cute too. Our fans are gonna *love* you."

Kalil smiled, blushing. "Thanks. So, does this mean I'm in?"

Harpo and Vi both turned to look through the door at Adder, who was behind the bar mixing some electric blue concoction that looked like glass cleaner. "You're in," Adder confirmed, glancing up long enough to shoot Kalil a smoldering look from beneath those long black lashes. He poured the neon-colored liquid from the huge plastic pitcher into four extra-large plastic Aqua Teen Hunger Force cups. "Let's celebrate. Drinks are on me."

Vi walked over, picked up one of the cups and sniffed it. "What is this?"

"I don't know." Adder grinned, eyes sparkling. "But it's got that blue stuff and an absolutely sinful quantity of tequila, so it's got to be good."

"Smells like it could clean the grease off your driveway." Harpo narrowed his eyes at it, shrugged and took a huge swallow. He shuddered. "Oh, man. That's evil."

Adder slinked out from behind the bar, swayed over to Kalil and handed him a cup of the bright blue stuff. Kalil took it, raised the cup in a silent toast and drank. The liquor burned its way to his stomach. "Good stuff," he gasped, eyes watering.

"Mmmmm." Adder linked his arm through Kalil's and steered him toward the sofa against the wall. They plopped down side by side, and Adder promptly scooted closer until his thigh pressed against Kalil's. "So. Are you named after the drug, or the cereal?"

It took a moment for Kalil to work out what Adder meant. When he did, he shot a glare at Harpo, who grinned and waved from the bar where he stood talking to Vi. "Neither. I have dyslexia, and it wasn't diagnosed until my senior year."

The light dawned in Adder's eyes. "Oooooh. Special *classes.* I get it."

"Nobody calls me Special K anymore."

"Of course not." Adder's gaze took a slow, thorough tour of Kalil's body. When he arrived back at Kalil's face, his smile had turned seductive. "You're a beautiful man, Special K."

For the first time ever, Kalil was glad to hear his despised high school nickname, because it killed the urge to flirt back. "I hope me being your drummer isn't contingent on me sleeping with you, because I'm not gonna."

"Straight?"

"Nope. I just don't sleep with bandmates."

"Too bad. I bet we'd be *really* hot together." With a deep sigh, Adder slouched against the sofa cushions. "Oh well. I guess you wouldn't really fit in with the band if you didn't reject me like the rest of them do."

Kalil snickered. "Somehow, I can't believe you have any trouble getting guys into bed."

"Hm, that's true. Boys, girls, they all want me. All except the people I want the most." Adder raised his face and aimed a brilliant smile at Vi, who'd wandered over. "Vi! My darling! Sit on Adder's lap, sweetheart." Adder grabbed Vi's wrist and tugged. She tumbled into his lap with a little shriek, sloshing a bit of her drink on his shirt.

Kalil took the opportunity to get up and join Harpo at the bar. He had a feeling Adder wasn't going to give up on trying to get him into bed, and he was horribly afraid he'd cave if he didn't get away for a while. Adder was damn near impossible to resist, in spite of the arrogance, the weird clothes and the general lack of shame.

"Hey, Isaac." Kalil set his cup on the bar and tugged on Harpo's sleeve. "Cut this thing with some soda, would you? I think it's already eating a hole through my stomach."

Harpo glared, and Kalil laughed. He had no sympathy. In his pre-blond-'fro days, Harpo had earned his *Love Boat*-inspired nickname in spades with nautical-style clothes and some seriously misguided facial hair.

"Ha ha, very fucking funny." Harpo skirted the end of the bar to dig through the shelves in back. He emerged with a bottle of club soda, opened it and poured a generous portion into both their drinks. "You better not resurrect that one. Harpo I am now, and Harpo I would like to remain."

"Hey, payback's a bitch." Kalil laughed at the apprehension on Harpo's face. "Dude, I'm just kidding. You don't call me Special K, I won't call you Isaac."

"Deal."

Harpo stuck out his hand. Kalil took it and they shook.

Full-throated laughter rang out behind them. Kalil turned around. Adder lay sprawled on his side on the sofa, his drink sitting on the floor and both arms wrapped around his belly. He was laughing so hard tears streaked down his cheeks. Vi sat beside him, giggling into her cup. They both looked very young and carefree. Kalil found the whole picture at once adorable and annoying.

Sitting up, Adder looped an arm around Vi's neck, pulled her close and kissed her. Kalil spun to face Harpo again. "I didn't know they were seeing each other." *He was just coming on to* me, *the whore.*

"They're not together. They just have sex sometimes, is all."

"But Adder said you and Vi both rejected him."

"My boy, Adder is deranged. You will learn this."

Kalil turned to peer over his shoulder. Vi and Adder had stopped kissing, for which Kalil was unaccountably relieved. Adder caught his eye with a saucy wink, and Kalil hastily turned away. "So. What's his story?"

"What do you mean?"

What *did* he mean? Not entirely sure himself, he settled on the question which was, irritatingly, topmost in his mind. "Is he always such a slut?"

Harpo laughed. "Yeah, pretty much." He cut a sly look at Kalil. "Adder loves to fuck, but he doesn't do commitment."

"Um. Okay, whatever." Forcing himself to not turn around and see what Adder was doing, Kalil took a sip of his neon-colored drink and grimaced. "What's his real name?"

"Adder."

"No it isn't."

"It is. Really."

Kalil remained unconvinced. "No way, dude. Who'd name their kid Adder?"

Harpo shrugged. "Nobody. But, it's Adder now. He had it legally changed last year."

Against his better judgment, Kalil sipped his drink again. It seemed to be getting more lethal every time. His sense of self-preservation made him set the cup down. "So what was his name before he changed it?"

Harpo grinned. "If I told you that, I'd have to kill you."

"C'mon, Harpo."

"Why are you so curious?"

Kalil frowned at a puddle of blue liquid on the bar. He wasn't sure exactly why he wanted to know more about Adder, but he had a sneaking suspicion it might be because he found the man irritatingly attractive. Not that he was telling Harpo that in this lifetime.

"I was just wondering what kind of freakazoid name he was born with, if it was so bad he changed it to *Adder*." At least that was true, even if it wasn't the whole truth.

Harpo's arched brow said he knew better, but he didn't argue. Unfortunately, he also didn't answer Kalil's question. Kalil was pondering the best way to approach Vi for answers when a pair of arms snaked around him from behind and a slick tongue lodged itself in his ear. He broke out of the unexpected embrace with a yelp.

He whirled around and met Adder's gleeful grin with a glare. "Don't *do* that."

The grin widened and edged over the border into evil. "You're going to be fun."

Ignoring the part of him that wanted to jump on Adder and shove his tongue right in the middle of that wicked smile, Kalil gathered the rags of his dignity around him and faced his new bandmate with an entirely fake calm. "So, when do we start practicing together? I know y'all play all the time, so I expect you have a show already scheduled soon."

Adder morphed from mischievous child to hardcore businessman so fast Kalil's head spun. "Actually, we have a gig next week at The Wedge. It's not a very large venue, but I want us to put on a show the whole city will talk about."

"We're after a show at The Tabernacle," Vi piped up. "If we can get in there, we have a great shot at bigger clubs all over the Southeast."

"And if we do that, maybe we can swing a festival gig," Harpo added, stirring his drink with his finger.

Adder nodded. "If we can get a spot in a festival, maybe Bonnaroo or Voodoo, we can catch the ear of a big-name band and thus get an opening spot on a tour. From there, it's only one step up to headlining."

Kalil blinked. "Wow. Y'all've really thought this through, huh?"

Adder gave him an indecipherable look. "Believe it or not, I take my career—*our* career—very seriously."

"I know," Kalil answered, feeling chastised. "Obviously you do."

"That's corrcct." Adder leaned closer. "Never underestimate my ambition, Special K. I want to be famous. And I *get* what I want." He pecked Kalil right on the lips, straightened up and tossed his hair out of his eyes. "Can you practice tomorrow, darling?"

"Uh... Um, yeah, sure." Kalil licked his lips, catching a taste of tequila. "What time?"

"Four to seven."

"Okay."

The dazzling smile that probably got Adder laid on a daily basis lit up his face. "Excellent. All right, my dears, I'm going to Little Five Points to shop, would anyone like to come along?"

Harpo let out a squeal that would've made Kalil doubt his straightness if he didn't know better. "Me! I need some new boots."

"Wonderful." Adder slung an arm around Harpo's neck. "Vi, we'll see you at home, love. Kalil, I will see you tomorrow at rehearsal."

Adder spun and strode off, dragging a protesting Harpo along by the neck. Kalil stared after them, feeling at once shocked and fiercely turned on. Both emotions irritated the living shit out of him. He absolutely could *not* let Adder's dangerous combination of sex appeal and relentless seduction wear him down. He'd traveled the bandmate-as-lover road before, and nothing good lay at the end of it.

A rather hard nudge in the ribs interrupted his thoughts. He turned to look at Vi, who was staring at him expectantly. "Sorry, what?" he said, embarrassed that he'd missed whatever she'd just said.

"I was just asking if you want to go with me to get a burger or something. I'm starved."

"Yeah, sure. That sounds like fun." Kalil's gaze drifted back to the door through which Adder and Harpo had gone.

Grinning, Vi nudged him again. "He's one of a kind, I know."

"Who?" Kalil asked, though he knew damn well who.

"Adder." Vi patted his shoulder. "Don't worry about it. He affects everyone that way. That's why everybody comes to our shows." She leaned around the side of the bar and emerged with a huge Betty Boop purse which she slung over her shoulder. "C'mon, let's go."

Kalil glanced at the half-empty cups sitting around the room. "Shouldn't we clean up first?"

Vi giggled. "Aw, you're so cute!"

Cute? Just because I'm not a slob? Kalil frowned. Vi laughed. "It's okay, we take turns picking up. It's my turn today, but I really need food first. I skipped breakfast and lunch, and my stomach's about to eat a hole in itself. I'll come back after and do the cleaning."

"Oh. Okay." He smiled at her. "I'll come back with you and help."

With an excited little squeal, she reached out and pulled him into a quick, one-armed hug. "That would be great, thanks."

"My pleasure."

Still beaming, Vi led the way down the hall and out into the alley. Kalil followed her, trying not to think about whether or not Adder dyed *all* his hair green.

Chapter Three

The gig at The Wedge surpassed Adder's wildest dreams. Kalil's energetic and inventive drum work added a richness which Adder hadn't even known had been missing from their music until now. The audience screamed twice as loud as usual and refused to let them go without two encores, which just proved that Adder's instincts were correct. Kalil was the perfect addition to their group. He was one of the best, most dedicated musicians Adder had ever known. Which was saying a great deal, considering how picky Adder was in who he considered to be a good musician.

Of course, from an audience-drawing perspective, it didn't hurt that the man was also a walking wet dream. Olive skin, big dark eyes, black hair that fell in a halo of wild waves around an androgynous face which wouldn't have been out of place on a Botticelli angel.

There was nothing androgynous about Kalil's body, though. Just one glimpse of those well-toned arms and that muscular back running with sweat was enough to make Adder's prick harden. He'd always had a weakness for a drummer's physique. Especially drummers who put everything they had into their jobs the way Kalil did.

Perched on a barstool at The Wedge after the lingering would-be groupies had been shooed away, Adder sipped his Kir

Royale and watched Kalil take down his drum kit. He disassembled each piece with the same care he'd used to put it together, every movement precise and careful. Adder couldn't help wondering if he touched his lovers with such reverence.

Probably not. Adder chuckled under his breath, amused with himself in spite of the sexual frustration caused by Kalil's unwavering refusal to fuck him. He had to admire a man who could make him wish to be a drum.

Harpo wandered out of the cramped hallway leading to the restrooms and plopped onto the barstool beside Adder. "This was a fucking *epic* show." He leaned his elbows on the bar behind him and flashed Adder a wide grin. "Man, we totally got it right hiring Kalil, huh?"

"Oh yes." Adder caught Kalil's eye and flicked his tongue out at him. Kalil scowled and turned back to his precious drums. "Gods, what I wouldn't give to get that man between my legs."

"You're a slut," Harpo told him, though there was no real heat in the accusation. He scratched his bare chest. "Seriously, Adder. He's fantastic live. The girls love him."

It was true. Once they'd introduced their new drummer to the tight-packed crowd, every wispy little Goth girl in the place seemed to osmose to the front row to worship Kalil in their near-silent, disturbingly intense way.

Adder had been a bit disconcerted by that at first. After all, *he* was the name and face of this band. All that attention should be *his*. Then he'd remembered that no matter how much those girls lusted after him, Kalil was not *ever* going to sleep with them, and he'd felt better. Plus the fanboys still seemed to focus mostly on Adder, which went a long way toward soothing his bruised ego.

Maybe he and Kalil could have a threesome with one of the

more attractive young men. *I wouldn't mind sharing with him,* Adder thought in a burst of magnanimous impulse. *Especially if he would fuck me.*

The mental image of himself impaled on Kalil's prick while sucking some faceless pretty boy's cock was a very nice one. Adder hummed into his glass.

A hard nudge from Harpo nearly knocked Adder off his barstool. He shot a frosty glare at Harpo, who just smirked. "Adder. Would you *please* stop trying to get K into bed? You're gonna drive him away."

Adder shook his head. "No. He wants me."

"Maybe, maybe not. But he's not into fucking his bandmates."

"We'll see about that."

Harpo let out an exasperated sigh. "C'mon, man. Don't you get enough ass already? Why do you have to go chasing after Kalil?"

Why, indeed? Adder had no answer for that question. There was no lack of men and women willing to fuck him. Hell, there'd been at least five girls and three guys in the first row tonight who would've gladly shared his bed for a few hours. A couple of them had been every bit as physically attractive as Kalil. But he'd ignored their transparent offers of no-strings sex in favor of a chance to be around Kalil for a while longer, a decision which he knew damn well would result in him jerking off in the shower later. So why had he done it? He had no clue, and that irked him beyond belief.

On stage, Kalil straightened up, linked his hands above his head and stretched. Adder stared, mesmerized by the damp skin of his naked chest and the tantalizing glimpse of sharp hipbones peeking above the waistband of his well-worn jeans. Gods, the man was a human kebab of ripe, tasty maleness.

Adder sipped his drink, imagining the tang of Kalil's sweat on his tongue.

Beside him, Harpo dropped his head into his hands and groaned. "Jesus, Adder. Could you at least try not to look like you're about to jump him any second?"

"I'm a passionate person. I can't help that." Adder waited until Kalil glanced his way, then licked the rim of his glass in a way that left no doubt as to what he'd rather be licking. Kalil went crimson and turned away, giving Adder a stunning view of his ass encased in body-hugging denim. "Besides, I do believe he enjoys my attentions."

"It makes him uncomfortable, asshole."

"Uncomfortable in an 'I have a hard-on that needs Adder's mouth immediately' way, perhaps."

Harpo sighed. "Adder, I swear to God if you fuck this up for us—"

"I will *not* fuck this up." Adder tore his gaze away from the object of his thus-far unrequited lust to aim a pointed look at Harpo. "This band is always first with me. You should know that by now."

"I know. It's just that sometimes I think you let your need to be loved cloud your judgment."

Adder's mouth fell open in shock. "Do not say the 'L' word to me," he sputtered when he thought he could talk again. "You *know* I don't believe in that."

"Yeah, that's what you keep telling me." Harpo stared at him, dark eyes searching. "Look, man, you're my friend. I care about you, and I'd like to see you happy. Just don't look for that inside the band, okay? It never ends well. For the band, or anyone else."

Stunned by his friend's unprecedented speech, Adder could

only stare in frustrating, humiliating silence. He didn't know which was worse—the fact that Harpo thought Adder was actually looking for *love*, or that he clearly believed Adder wasn't capable of it. *Of course* he could love someone, if he chose. He just didn't want to.

By the time he collected himself enough to come up with a scathing answer, Sheila had detached herself from Vi and was teetering across the floor toward them on her ridiculous three-inch heels. He forced his face to obey his will and gave her a beaming smile. "Sheila, my love! How did you like the show tonight?"

"It was good. Kalil rocks." She hooked her arm around Harpo's shoulders, leaned close and kissed him. "Can we go to my place tonight, babe? I'd like to be alone for a change." She shot a barbed glare at Adder, who fluttered his eyelashes at her.

Harpo studied Adder's face for several unnerving seconds, then nodded. "Okay, sure. Adder, you'll make sure Vi gets home okay, right? She rode with me."

"Of course I will. You kids go on, and have a good time." Adder winked at Sheila. "I'll miss you in Harpo's bed tonight, Sheila darling."

"Pig," Sheila muttered. She grabbed Harpo's arm so hard her hot pink nails dug into his skin. "Come on, Harmon. We're out of here."

Adder snickered. Harpo dealt a stinging blow to his shoulder before jumping off the barstool. "See you tomorrow, Adder."

"Until then." Adder waved at the retreating pair. He thought he could hear Harpo growling that he didn't care if Harmon was his real name, he hated when Sheila called him that.

Chuckling, Adder drained the last of his drink, set the glass on the bar and hopped to his feet. He glanced around. Vi and one of the Wedge staff—Susan? Sarah? Something with an "S"—stood huddled together in the corner of the club near the front door, evidently discussing something of vital importance. Another staff member whistled an off-key tune while he mopped beer and assorted other substances off the floor. Kalil zipped his favorite drumsticks into their special pouch, set it carefully on top of the bass drum and walked offstage.

Adder followed without hesitation. He could always pretend he'd been innocently heading for the men's to take a piss.

When he reached the dressing room, Kalil was already bent over the sofa. Adder stared in pleased surprise. Then he realized Kalil wasn't offering him a fuck, he was searching for something in the cushions. Undeterred in spite of his disappointment, Adder wandered over and perched on the sofa's arm. "Hi, Special K."

Kalil shot him the fiery glare that always made his blood sing. "Will you *please* stop calling me that?"

"What are you looking for?" Adder inquired, ignoring Kalil's request since he had no intention of honoring it.

"I had twenty dollars in my pocket when we got here, and now I can't find it." With a deep sigh, Kalil straightened up and ran both hands through his dripping hair. "Hell, maybe I just thought I had it. Maybe I left it at home."

"That's possible. Haven't we all done things like that sometimes?" Adder watched a drop of sweat wind its way between Kalil's pecs and down the middle of his abdomen. "Gods, I really want to lick you all over right now."

Kalil scowled. "Quit it, Adder."

Adder grinned. Kalil turned away, but not fast enough. The flush in his cheeks and the sudden swell in the front of his jeans just confirmed what Adder already knew. Kalil wanted him. Badly.

Considering that the feeling was mutual, Adder saw no reason not to act on it. They were alone for a change, and he'd behaved for *so* long already. He stood, grabbed Kalil's arm, whirled him around and pulled him close with an arm around his waist.

It was intoxicating, feeling Kalil's body pressed tight against his. Kalil's bare chest was warm and damp, his brown eyes wide with shock and a need he couldn't disguise. Adder leaned close and drew a deep breath. The scent of sweat and desire flooded his brain. Unable to stop himself—not that he would have tried in any case—he slid a hand into Kalil's hair, tilted his face up and kissed him.

Kalil's mouth opened on a little kittenish whimper, his body melting into Adder's embrace. For a heart-stopping second, Adder thought he might actually get away with it. Then Kalil stiffened and shoved out of Adder's arms. "What the fuck, dude?"

He was obviously trying to sound outraged, but the lust in his voice drowned out the indignation. Adder smiled. "I've been wanting to do that since the first time I saw you. So I did it."

"Yeah, well." Kalil clasped his hands in front of his crotch in a transparent—and unsuccessful—attempt to hide the erection Adder had felt against his thigh mere moments before. "Did you ever stop to think maybe I didn't want you to?"

"No." Adder laughed at Kalil's incredulous expression. "Come on, Kalil. You *want* me. Don't pretend you don't."

"God, you're just..." With a frustrated growl, Kalil snatched his crumpled shirt off the sofa, shoved past Adder and stomped into the hall.

Adder didn't follow. Crowding Kalil right now would be counterproductive. He needed time to come to terms with their mutual attraction. Adder would gladly give him that time, if it meant getting him into bed in the end. And Adder was certain it would mean exactly that.

Lifting both hands, Adder buried his face in his palms and breathed deep. He could smell Kalil on his skin, sweat and musk and cheap shampoo. The scent made his head spin and his belly tighten. The feeling had gotten to be very familiar in the week and a half since they'd hired Kalil. Which was a bit disconcerting, when Adder thought about it. His past lovers had never affected him as strongly as Kalil did just by being near. What the hell did it mean, Adder wondered, that he was so obsessed with getting Kalil to fuck him?

He didn't know the answer to that and wasn't sure he wanted to.

Pushing the uncomfortable thoughts to the back of his mind, Adder retrieved the messenger bag he'd stashed behind the sofa and sauntered out of the dressing room. Maybe he could entice Vi into sharing his bed tonight. It wouldn't be the same as spending the night with Kalil, but it was better than sleeping alone.

Chapter Four

Two weeks after their success at The Wedge, the manager of The Tabernacle called to offer them a prime Saturday night spot for the very next weekend. Adder was smugly pleased that everything was going according to his master plan. Kalil, however, couldn't work up Adder's level of enthusiasm about it.

"We only got this gig because Little Boy Blue had to cancel," Kalil said, not for the first time, as he and Adder sat on a downtown bench sharing a box of chili fries while they waited for Vi to pick them up. He popped a chili-laden fry into his mouth and chewed, savoring the spicy taste. "Doesn't that bother you any?"

Adder shrugged. "Not really, no."

"Why not?"

"Why does it matter?"

Kalil took a sip of his iced tea. "I'd just rather people hired us because we're *good*, not because we're available."

Turning sideways to face Kalil, Adder bent one long leg and planted his red suede boot on the bench. "K, my love, we know how good we are. Our fans know how good we are. The Tabernacle management will soon learn how good we are, if they're not already aware of it, which they probably are. They don't generally hire anyone, no matter how available they are, without making sure they're worthy first."

"Yeah, I guess you're probably right." Kalil snagged another fry from the box. "It still bothers me, though."

"Don't let it bother you." Adder reached over and brushed a stray curl from Kalil's face. "It doesn't matter why they hired us. All that matters is they *did*. We are going to be playing at one of the city's most popular clubs. That means a bigger audience, and new fans."

"That's true." Kalil let out a relieved breath when Adder stopped touching him. He had trouble keeping his hands to himself when Adder played with his hair like that. "You know what?"

"What?"

Kalil shook his head when Adder's tongue flicked around the tip of his straw. "You're the most amoral person I've ever met."

Adder's eyes widened. "What do you mean?"

"You don't care *how* you get famous, as long as you're famous." Kalil scooped up chili with one finger and licked it off. "And you sleep around so much it's a wonder you don't have a dozen kinds of social disease by now."

"How do you know I don't?" Adder murmured, watching Kalil's mouth with a hunger he didn't even try to hide.

Kalil shrugged. "Just a guess."

The gleefully evil smile which always made Kalil's stomach turn cartwheels spread over Adder's face. "You're right, as it happens. I am as healthy as the proverbial horse."

Hung like one too. Kalil kept *that* observation to himself. The last thing he needed was Adder finding out just how often Kalil had visually mapped the outline of his prick through the thin, clingy clothes he tended to wear.

"I always insist on condoms," Adder continued, seemingly

oblivious to Kalil's fixation on his genitals. "And I get tested regularly. *And*, I made sure to get my Hepatitis B vaccine." He leaned a little too close for comfort, a sly smile curving that wicked mouth and making Kalil think, inevitably, of The Kiss. "What about you, my sweet Special K? Are you careful? Do you take care of that gorgeous, sexy body of yours?"

Kalil couldn't help the smile that spread over his face, or the laughter that bubbled up. Adder might be an annoying, melodramatic man-child with an ego the size of China—on second thought, there was no "might" about it, he most definitely was all those things—but something about him made it impossible to stay mad at him. Which was good, because without that intangible quality Kalil probably would've killed him after The Kiss. It had taken Kalil three whole days to get his desire for his bandmate under some semblance of control again after that.

"Don't you ever give up?" Kalil teased, grinning.

Adder arched an eyebrow at him. "You know me better than that."

Kalil snorted. "Yeah, I guess I do."

Eyes sparkling behind his round, pale pink sunglasses, Adder inclined his body forward enough to invade the hell out of Kalil's personal space. "Which means," Adder purred, "that you may as well give in now." He dipped his head to rub his smooth cheek against Kalil's. "I'll have you, my darling. My shy, beautiful Kalil. One day, I'll have you."

A shiver ran up Kalil's back. Summoning every ounce of strength he had, he gripped Adder's shoulders with both hands and pushed him firmly away. "No, Adder, you won't. Stop it."

Adder drew back enough to look Kalil in the eye. Kalil dropped his hands and silently pleaded with any higher powers out there to *please* make Adder behave just this once. The infuriating bastard didn't always stop when Kalil told him to, and resisting his advances had become a monumental effort for Kalil ever since that tantalizing taste of how it might be between them. The last thing he needed was to be arrested for public sex, so he *really* hoped this would be one of those rare times when Adder actually listened to him.

Apparently it was his lucky day. Adder shrugged, leaned back on one hand and turned his attention to the chili fries as if he hadn't been trying to get into Kalil's pants for the five thousandth time that week. Kalil breathed a sigh of relief.

"You never answered my question." Adder held out the box. "Do you want the rest?"

"You didn't ask me that." Kalil pressed three of the remaining fries together and used them to scoop up a pile of chili. He stuffed the whole business into his mouth.

"Manners of an ox." Sighing, Adder rested his chin on his bent knee. "I meant, you never answered my other question."

"What other question?" Kalil picked up his cup, then put it down again with a grimace when nothing but air came through the straw. "Can I have some of your drink? Mine's all gone."

Adder handed him the soda and watched with an unusually solemn expression as he polished it off. "I asked you if you're careful. If you take the proper precautions when you have sex."

Yeah, I'm so fucking careful I haven't gotten laid in months. Not that I'm telling him that. Kalil forced a casual smile. "Yep. Rubbers, testing, the whole thing."

"Good. I'd hate to think of anything bad happening to you."

Surprised by this unexpected seriousness, Kalil stared. Before he could recover enough to say anything else, though, Adder jumped to his feet and started gathering their trash. "There's Vi's car. Let's go."

Kalil followed Adder down the sidewalk to the corner where Vi's old purple Buick waited. For the life of him, he couldn't think of a thing to say. This was the first time Adder had ever expressed anything for Kalil other than pure lust or professional respect. It was strange, and a whole hell of a lot harder to ignore than Adder's usual flirting, innuendo and blatant offers of sex. It made it seem like Adder actually *cared* about him. Like maybe he saw Kalil as more than a fellow musician and potential fuck-buddy.

He's probably just starting to see you as a friend, Kalil mused as Adder tossed their takeout box and the drink cups into a trash can beside the "walk" signal. *Nothing wrong with that. If you're friends, maybe he'll quit trying to get you into bed.*

Of course, all available evidence suggested otherwise. Harpo and Vi were Adder's closest friends, and he came on to both of them all the time. In Vi's case, his attempts even succeeded occasionally.

Sighing, Kalil climbed into the front seat beside Vi. If she and Harpo could still be friends with Adder in spite of his obsession with sex, then Kalil could too. All he had to do was keep saying "no".

He tried not to think of his growing desire to say "yes" instead.

Kalil woke to a dry, furry tongue and a fierce pain trying to jackhammer his skull apart. He groped along the side of his head with one hand. His brain did not appear to be leaking out his ears, which must mean he had the worst hangover in the history of the universe.

Leaving his hand over his face to block out the light

bleeding red through his closed eyelids, he lay as still as humanly possible and tried to piece together just what the hell he'd done the night before. He and the band had put on a totally historic show at The Tabernacle, after which Adder had taken everyone out for celebratory drinks at a dim, grungy, very loud hole-in-the-wall bar somewhere in the depths of Midtown.

The last thing Kalil recalled with any clarity was knocking back several shots of tequila. Everything after that only came back to him in flashes.

Laughter. Music. The press of bodies all around, moving like it was the end of the world and they only had a few hours to dance a lifetime's worth. A lean frame pressing against his chest. Long arms around him, fingers drawing patterns on the small of his back. Smells of liquor and sweat. Hazel eyes dark and heavy with lust. Soft lips, softer tongue. A hand between his legs. A proposition, an acceptance. Adder's smile shining bright as the sun as they left the bar together.

Wait. Together?

Kalil thought about it. Yes, they'd left together. No Harpo. No Vi. Just Kalil and Adder, stumbling down the street with their arms around each other.

Oh shit. What the fuck did I do?

Kalil cracked one eye open and peered between his fingers, wincing as the sunlight pouring through the open curtains tried to slice his head open. He saw a scarred and battered wooden table, a white clock-radio and an open closet with an overflowing laundry basket inside before the pain forced his eyes shut again.

At least he was in his own apartment. Maybe the part about leaving with Adder—not to mention the fuzzy mental images of earth-shaking, mind-melting sex—was just his overactive imagination. He'd indulged in enough Adder-centered fantasies lately that the idea of him dreaming the whole thing wasn't too farfetched.

Behind him, something hummed. The mattress moved. An arm slipped around his middle and a warm, naked body molded itself to his back. "Good morning, beautiful," Adder's sleep-rough voice murmured in his ear. "Or afternoon, rather. Mmmm, I slept like a baby in your bed."

Fuck. I didn't dream it. Kalil groaned. He couldn't decide if the gymnastics going on in his stomach were brought on by too much alcohol or Adder's dick nestled in the crease of his ass. "Please tell me we didn't do what I think we did."

"Sorry, darling, but we did. Repeatedly." Adder's hand wandered down Kalil's belly. He wound a curl of Kalil's pubic hair around one finger and gave a gentle tug. "You were magnificent."

"Oh God."

"Mmm, that's what you kept screaming last night when I was fucking you."

Mortified, Kalil pressed the heel of his hand to his splitting forehead. "Jesus fucking Christ, I can't believe I had sex with you."

"I can't believe you don't remember it. Ah, the dangers of too much alcohol." Adder nuzzled Kalil's neck. "But then again, if you hadn't had so much to drink, I doubt you would've been quite so...uninhibited." The clever, evil fingers slid out of Kalil's pubes to worm between his thighs. "Let's do it again. You can fuck me this time."

Kalil about jumped out of his skin when Adder's thumb stroked the head of his cock. Ignoring Adder's grasping hands, Kalil shoved himself out of Adder's embrace and into a sitting position. He stumbled out of bed, slipped on a used condom, banged his knee on the bedside table and finally fetched up against the wall. Agony exploded through his skull, which in this case was a good thing because it nearly drowned out all the other aches and pains which flared to life with his sudden movement. He knew why his ass was so sore—*oh my God, Adder fucked me; shit, shit, shit*—but he had no idea why the rest of him throbbed like he'd just finished the Ironman, and wasn't sure he wanted to know.

"I think you should go home now." Kalil leaned against the wall, one arm around his protesting belly and the other holding his head on. "Fucking hell. Remind me to never, ever drink again."

Shaking his head, Adder slid out of bed with far more grace than Kalil had. He stalked forward like a panther. "My dear Special K. You are *not* going to stand there and tell me this was a mistake, are you? That you didn't enjoy having my cock inside you?" Adder pressed both hands onto the wall on either side of Kalil's head. "Because I know you did." A sly grin curved Adder's red and swollen mouth. "You were quite *vocal* about that."

Kalil scowled. His jaw ached almost as much as his rear end, and his throat felt raw, which probably meant Adder was right. Kalil had always been a screamer. The few hazy memories he was able to stir up from the depths of last night's inebriation told him he had indeed enjoyed himself. A lot.

Dammit.

With a pathetic little whimper, Kalil slid down the wall to sit on the floor. He rested his forehead on his drawn-up knees. "Look, obviously we were both pretty drunk last night—"

"I wasn't."

Kalil lifted his head long enough to glare, then put it down again when Adder just winked at him. "Well, I was. *Very* drunk. My judgment was crap. Yes, I'm physically attracted to you. But

I did not want to sleep with you."

"Yes, you did."

I will not kill him. Maybe another day. Not right now. "Sexual attraction and willingness to have sex are not the same thing." Inspiration struck, and Kalil went with it before he could overanalyze it. "I only had sex with you because I was drunk. Is that really what you want? Someone you can only fuck if they're too shitfaced to know what they're doing? Can't you do better than that?"

Silence. Kalil lifted his head and stole a cautious look at Adder's face. His expression was thoughtful. Kalil held still and waited, doing his best not to stare slack-jawed at Adder's nude body. It was a very nice body, tall and slim with smooth, streamlined muscles. He'd seen Adder nearly naked on stage, of course. The man was a shameless exhibitionist and loved to strip to his underwear during their performances, but this was the first time Kalil had seen him without at least his skimpy green Lycra shorts. Not counting last night, which Kalil didn't completely remember anyway.

He couldn't help noticing Adder's groin was shaved bare. The snake tattoo wound all the way up his thigh to the base of his cock. The snake's fangs formed inked dents at the juncture of groin and shaft, and the forked tongue corkscrewed the length of the shaft to tickle the head.

Kalil bit back the urge to lick it. He had a sinking feeling he'd already done that.

"You're right," Adder declared, shocking Kalil out of his perusal of Adder's privates. "I can do better."

"Oh. Uhhh..." Kalil blinked up at Adder. "Yeah. Good."

Adder laughed. "Oh, my lovely Kalil. If you could only see the way you're looking at me right now." He cupped his balls in one hand, wrapped the other around his prick and wiggled his hips. "Are you sure you wouldn't like just one more taste of my cock?"

Kalil swallowed. "Yes. I mean, yes, I'm sure," he clarified when Adder's smile turned lecherous. "Would you please just leave now? *Please.*"

To his surprise, Adder nodded. "All right."

Not quite believing his good luck—*it* is *good luck, of course it is*—Kalil studied Adder while he plucked his clothes from the pile on the floor. "So. We're okay, right? I mean, as far as the band."

Adder pinned him with an indecipherable look. Kalil ran a nervous hand through his hair. God, if sleeping with Adder got him kicked out of the best band he ever been in, he'd didn't know what he'd do.

"We're fine," Adder said, *finally*, his voice soft. He shrugged into his vivid yellow cardigan. "I've told you over and over again that us having sex wouldn't have any effect on the band. You'll see that I'm right."

"Yeah. Well. Good." Kalil watched with some disappointment as Adder's tattoo disappeared under a pair of red sequined pants.

Grinning as if he knew exactly what Kalil was thinking, Adder slipped on his sneakers, slinked over to Kalil, grabbed his hands and pulled him to his feet. "Sleep until you feel better, darling. I'll see you tomorrow at practice."

"Uh-huh." Kalil told himself he was only leaning against Adder's chest because he was so dizzy he'd probably fall over if he didn't. "Four o'clock, right?"

"Right." Before Kalil quite knew what was happening, Adder lifted his chin and kissed him.

Kalil knew he shouldn't allow it to happen. He should push

Adder away and tell him off. But he didn't. He opened his mouth and let Adder's tongue find his, in spite of mutual morning-after-a-drinking-binge breath. He liked to think he gave Adder his way because it would get rid of him faster, rather than because it felt so damn good.

"Goodbye, my sweet Kalil," Adder whispered, stroking Kalil's cheek. "Next time we make love, it'll be when we're both sober. I'm looking forward to that."

Next time?

Too stunned to answer, Kalil gaped as Adder released him, turned and walked out the door without a backward glance. He'd thought that Adder would at least stop coming on to him now that he'd gotten what he'd been chasing all this time. Evidently not. It seemed that Kalil would have to keep fighting him off, only it would be harder than ever now that he knew—kind of—what he'd been missing.

Groaning, Kalil let his head fall forward into his hands. What the fuck was he going to do now?

Chapter Five

"Ladies and gentlemen, thank you from the bottom of our hearts. Good night!"

Adder waved at the solid sea of humanity on the club floor, then floated off stage on a surge of screams and applause. The adoration of the audience was a feast for a starving soul. And gods, he needed that now more than he ever had. Lately he felt like performing was the only thing keeping him from a mental breakdown.

Kalil brushed past, soaking wet and smelling of hardworking man. It was all Adder could do to keep from grabbing him and running his hands all over that beautiful body. Especially now that he knew exactly how Kalil looked when he came.

That inscrutable dark-eyed gaze met Adder's for a split second before Kalil continued on to the dressing room. Adder barely held back a frustrated sigh. After three long weeks, he hadn't yet been able to convince Kalil to sleep with him again, and it bothered him more than he liked to admit.

What bothered him even more was that he still *wanted* it so badly. He'd had Kalil once. That should be enough. It always had been before. Why was this so different?

Vi dug an elbow into his ribs as she joined him in the wings. "Hey. Did you see who was in the audience tonight?"

Grateful for the distraction from confusing and distressing thoughts, Adder wound an arm around Vi's shoulders and kissed the top of her head. "Who was it this time, love? Elton John? Bono? Al Sharpton?"

She gave him a withering look. He laughed. The dear girl was always seeing celebrities in the crowd lately. Once she'd even sworn she'd spotted Bill Clinton in the balcony of a Charlotte, North Carolina venue. Not that it was impossible she was right. Since the Tabernacle show, "Pixie Dust" had become the savage queen of America's download jungle. In the southeast, anyway. The band had quickly outgrown the small clubs they used to play and started filling much larger venues. Why shouldn't famous people attend their shows? But even Adder had to admit it was pretty unlikely.

"You're an ass," Vi informed him, punctuating her opinion with a hard smack on his butt. "I'm serious here."

"I'm sorry, sweetness." He gave her a squeeze. "Tell me."

She glanced around, then stood on tiptoe to put her mouth close to his ear. "Jordan Rivers."

Surprised, he drew back enough to scan her face. She seemed perfectly serious. "You're certain?"

"Yeah, totally." Vi hooked a thumb in the waistband of Adder's shorts and started steering him toward the dressing rooms in the back of the club. "In fact, I thought I saw her at the bar when we played The Orange Peel on Thursday, but I didn't get a real good look so I wasn't sure. This time? I am. It was her."

Adder didn't answer. His brain was too busy turning over the possible reasons why one of the most powerful music promoters in the country would come to see them play. He couldn't come up with any explanation which didn't mean very, very good things for him and his band.

Harpo and Kalil were in the dressing room changing when Adder and Vi walked in. Harpo took one look at Adder's face and dropped the shirt he'd been about to pull over his head. "What happened?"

Adder raised his eyebrows. "What do you mean?"

"He means, you look like Sylvester would if he ever caught Tweety." Kalil plopped into a chair, swabbing the sweat off his face with a small blue towel. "So, what happened?"

Letting go of Vi, Adder stalked across the room and sprawled on the sofa. "Vi saw Jordan Rivers in the audience tonight."

Harpo snorted. "Sure she did."

"I did, jackass." Picking up her water bottle, Vi twisted off the cap and threw it at Harpo.

Adder interrupted before Harpo could snipe back and start a real fight. "If Vi was mistaken, it hurts no one. But what if she *wasn't* mistaken? What if she was right, and Jordan Rivers really was here tonight?" He scraped a bit of crusted dirt off his right knee with his thumbnail. "I think we have to consider that possibility."

"Hm." Kalil leaned forward, elbows resting on his knees, and looked directly at Adder for the first time in what felt like eons. "I think you're right. If she really was here tonight, she must've come specifically to see us. And if she did that..."

Adder nodded when Kalil trailed off. "Yes, exactly."

They stared at each other. The noise from the club and the sound of Vi and Harpo whispering together faded into the background. At that moment, Adder wanted more than anything in the world to pull Kalil to the floor and take him right there. He literally had to sit on his hands to keep himself from doing it.

Kalil's eyes flicked downward. One corner of his mouth hitched up, and Adder felt a vertiginous rush of desire. He drew a silent, shaking breath. Gods, but Kalil was going to kill him.

A rap on the dressing room door jolted Adder out of his lustful daze. Blinking, he forced his gaze from Kalil's lovely facc to the scarred and paint-splattered door.

"C'mon in," Vi called.

The door swung open to admit a curvy middle-aged woman with short, spiky blonde hair and pale green eyes sharp enough to cut a person to the bone. "Sorry to intrude. I won't be long. I just wanted to introduce myself and see if I could set up a meeting with you kids." Striding across the floor, she held out a manicured hand to Adder. "I'm Jordan Rivers."

"I know." Adder rose to his feet, took her hand and shook. "I'm Adder. This is Kalil Sabatino, Violet McGill and Harpo Hall." He gestured toward each of his bandmates in turn. "Thank you for coming to see our show, Ms. Rivers. I hope you enjoyed it."

"I did. Very much." Dropping Adder's hand, she turned her wide, toothy smile to the others in the room. "In fact, I've enjoyed your last *five* shows. You are an incredible live band."

Adder flashed her his most charming smile. "Thank you very much, Ms. Rivers."

She gave Adder an appreciative once-over. When her gaze met his again, it had become warmer than one would think necessary for a business-related conversation. "Call me Jordan."

Adder decided not to discourage her subtle flirting. Jordan Rivers was a very important person in the music world, and Adder wasn't above manipulating her attraction to him if the opportunity presented itself. He allowed a hint of seduction into his expression. "Again, thank you. Jordan."

"So, Ms. Rivers—"

"Jordan." She turned to face Kalil, who had risen from his chair and stood with arms crossed and a faint frown on his face. "Please. I don't like to stand on formalities."

Kalil's face relaxed a fraction, though his eyes still sparked with something Adder would've called anger if there were any reason for such a thing. "Okay. Jordan. We're thrilled that you like our music, but I'm wondering why exactly you're here."

To Adder's left, Vi let out a soft gasp. Harpo grabbed her hand. "Uh. What he meant was—"

"I'm sure he meant exactly what he said," Jordan broke in. Her smile didn't fade one iota, but her eyes took on an amused gleam. "Believe me, you'd have to try a lot harder than that to offend me, or make me angry. I appreciate Kalil's honesty." She returned her attention to Adder. "I'll get straight to the point. I'm putting together a new music festival, to be held this coming May in the Research Triangle area of North Carolina. I'd like to hire you and your band to play."

Adder managed, via a level of self-control he hadn't known he possessed, to avoid leaping into the air and whooping like a child. He'd expected to get a spot in a festival at some point, but not this soon. The offer was a delightful surprise, one he had every intention of accepting. A new festival didn't have quite the same prestige as an established one, but he wasn't about to turn down an opportunity this good for such a small reason.

"We'll need more details before we decide." His voice sounded calm and in control, for which he was profoundly grateful. "Could we meet another time to talk over the particulars?"

"Of course." Reaching into the pocket of her plum-colored jacket, she drew out a silver cardcase. She opened it, plucked out a business card and handed it to Adder. "Call my office tomorrow. My secretary has my schedule, he'll set up a meeting for you. Would you be available in the next few days? I'll be in Atlanta for about another week before I head back to New York."

"I'm sure that will be fine." A rush of giddy excitement made Adder's head spin. He grinned, unable to help himself. "Thank you very much, Jordan."

"My pleasure. It was wonderful meeting all of you. I hope we'll see each other again soon." Her gaze lingered on his face for a moment before she spun on one elegant black heel and walked out the door.

Stunned silence settled over the room in the wake of Jordan's departure. For a few seconds, they all just stood there staring at each other. Then Vi let out a squeal. "Oh my God, y'all. Did you *hear* that? We're gonna play a festival!"

"A brand new one too. They'll only hire the best because they have a reputation to build." Grabbing Vi around the waist, Harpo whirled her around. "Fuckin' A, man."

"We need to learn more before we accept this offer." Adder knew the ecstatic grin on his face sort of overrode the reminder, but he couldn't help it. They were going to play this festival. All that remained was to work out the details.

"It's exciting, sure. But I'm holding off on getting all worked up about it until we know more." Snatching his shirt off the arm of the sofa, Kalil pulled it on. "I don't know about the rest of you, but I'm beat. Let's get our stuff together and go home."

Adder frowned. In the past few weeks, he'd learned that Kalil was by far the most cautious member of the band. That he would feel a bit of trepidation about Jordan's offer was to be expected. Still, Adder could find no good reason for the barely controlled fury surrounding Kalil like a dark aura.

Glancing sideways, Adder caught Vi's gaze. She shook her head, and Adder stifled a frustrated sigh. At least he wasn't imagining Kalil's attitude.

He laid a hand on Kalil's arm as he strode past, stopping him in his tracks. "Kalil, what's wrong?"

"Nothing. I'm just tired, I want to go home, and I can't do that until we're done breaking down. So if you don't mind..." He shook off Adder's hand and walked out the door. He never once looked at Adder, or anyone else.

Harpo gazed after him, brows drawn together. "Huh. What the fuck's the matter with him?"

"I'd have thought you'd be able to tell *us* that," Adder said.

"Yeah, well, he can be kind of moody, especially when he's upset or confused about something, but I don't know what that could be right now." Harpo shrugged. "Whatever it is, he'll work it out and he'll be fine. That's how it's always been."

"Good. I hope so." Adder raked his sweaty hair out of his eyes. "All right, my loves. What say we follow our dear Special K's example and get our equipment together?"

Vi nodded. "Sure. Hey, I'm meeting Chrissy and Jonas at Charo's at two, Malignant Dwarf is supposed to be playing a secret show there. Y'all wanna come?"

"I do." Harpo linked his arm through Vi's. "What about it, Adder?"

Adder wrinkled his nose. Vi's friends were nice enough people, but he couldn't stand Malignant Dwarf. They were competent musicians, but any band who went out of their way to avoid any and all publicity was, in Adder's opinion, hypocritical and undeserving of his attention.

"No, thank you," he answered politely. "I've been out every night this week. I need my beauty sleep."

"Suit yourself." Vi tugged on Harpo's arm. "Come on, let's get the work done so we can go have fun. Adder, you can take the van, since you're going straight home."

The three of them left the dressing room. Adder trailed behind his two friends, his brain whirling. His excitement over landing a festival gig was tempered by Kalil's less-than-enthusiastic reaction. He knew Kalil wanted it as much as the rest of the band. They'd talked about it more than once. So why did Kalil seem so angry?

Adder had no idea. But he intended to find out.

The Atlanta office of Rivers Promotions was far less intimidating than Adder had thought it would be. He'd expected a top-floor suite in the business district. An overabundance of glass, chrome and black leather. Perhaps a few Pollack prints on the walls.

The funky Castleberry Hill loft came as a pleasant surprise. A tremendous arched window overlooked the bustling street two stories below. Sunlight flooded in to gild the plush red sofa and deep purple chairs which formed the waiting area. Bright splatters of paint dotted the wood-plank floor, and three stained-glass lights hung from the high ceiling on black chains. On the other side of the room, the secretary—an impossibly gorgeous young man with blue hair and a diamond stud in his nose—sat behind an antique oak desk, tapping away at the keyboard of his flat-screen computer. The wall behind him had obviously been added on to the original room. Jordan's private office lay beyond the bright blue door.

"This place is really cool," Vi whispered, lifting one corner of the red and gold throw rug with the toe of her shoe.

Grinning, Adder nudged Vi's knee with his. "You can speak out loud, my dear."

She pinched his thigh. "Shut up."

He laughed. The secretary glanced at him with a slight frown. Adder winked at him, and he turned away, porcelain cheeks flushing pink.

Kalil's booted foot kicked him in the shin. "Would you stop flirting with everything that moves for a little while, please?"

"But it's so much fun." Adder gave Kalil a sly smile. "Are you jealous, darling?"

The way Kalil's face flamed told Adder he'd hit a nerve. Kalil dropped his gaze and stared resolutely at the knee of his black jeans. "In about two minutes we have a meeting with a person who could possibly make our career. I just think a little professionalism would be a good thing here."

Before Adder could answer, Jordan's door opened and she leaned around the frame. "Guys? You can come in now."

The four of them stood and crossed the room to where Jordan waited. As he passed the desk, Adder bent to brush his lips against the adorable secretary's ear. "Sorry, my sweet, but I'm afraid you and I aren't going to happen." He cut his eyes sideways toward Kalil, who was staring with his mouth open. "My lover is the jealous type, sadly."

The blue-haired boy gaped. Kalil sputtered. Adder laughed. He shouldn't bait Kalil that way, he knew, but how could he resist when the man was so wonderfully easy to ruffle?

Taking Kalil's hand before he could protest, Adder led him into Jordan's office. Kalil wrenched free of Adder's grip and stood as far from Adder as possible. Adder took one of the two chairs in the small office and pretended to ignore the heat of Kalil's glare boring into the side of his head.

Once they'd all settled into place—Adder and Harpo in the chairs, Vi clutching Kalil's arm in the corner—Jordan beamed at them from across the desk. "Gentlemen, Ms. McGill, I'm very glad you're considering helping my partners and me launch the TART Festival this spring."

Harpo's eyebrows rose. "TART?"

"Triangle Arts, Rhythm and Transcendence." Jordan looked faintly embarrassed. "Some of our most important backers are into transcendental meditation. They wanted TM included in the program and in the title, so we obliged them."

"That sounds cool to me," Vi said.

"We're hoping it will add an extra dimension to the festival, and bring in more people." Opening the desk drawer to her right, Jordan took out four thick folders. She handed one to each of them. "These packets contain copies of our standard contract, plus a summary of all the salient points in plain language instead of legalese. I'll go over the details of the festival itself and your part in it, including payment, now. I expect you'll want a lawyer to review the contract before making your decision. Go ahead and do that. Make sure you're comfortable with everything. I'll need a decision one way or another within a month. We'll discuss any changes you'd like in the contract at that time. Sound good?"

Adder nodded along with his bandmates. "Thank you very much for preparing this information for us, Jordan. I wasn't expecting this level of consideration, to be honest."

Jordan leveled a steamy look at him. "To misquote one of my favorite movies, I believe this could be the beginning of a beautiful relationship." She tilted her head, a coy smile on her lips. "With your wonderful band, of course."

"Of course." Leaning forward, Adder planted his elbows on her desk and gazed into her eyes. "So. Tell us all about this festival of yours, darling."

By the time they left the office half an hour later, folders in hand, Adder could practically see the steam coming out of Kalil's ears. Kalil marched ahead of the rest of the group, his back stiff and his luscious mouth pressed into an angry line. He refused to so much as look at Adder during the MARTA ride from Jordan's office to the studio, where they'd left their cars.

Jealous, oh yes he is. Adder flashed a predatory grin at Kalil as they walked into the studio. Kalil favored him with a dagger-sharp glare which, perversely enough, made Adder's cock twitch and start to fill.

He licked his lips and stared shamelessly at the curve of Kalil's shoulder beneath the snug red T-shirt. Gods. He'd behaved for such a long, long time. He'd wanted Kalil to come to *him* this time, not the other way around. Nothing chafed Adder quite like coming off as desperate. But when it came to Kalil, he *was* desperate. Pathetically so. There was no way around it, and he could no longer deny it to himself.

He couldn't hold off any longer. He had to have Kalil again, and if he had to use the man's blatant jealousy of Jordan to have him, he'd do it.

His mind made up, Adder sauntered over to Kalil, who was gathering the things he'd left at the studio after practice that morning. "Hello, sweetness."

Kalil sighed. "What do you want, Adder?"

"Me and Harpo are out of here, guys," Vi called before Adder could answer. "See y'all later."

"Goodbye, love." Adder waved, ignoring Harpo's glower. Surely Harpo could see that Kalil wanted this as much as Adder did.

The studio door squealed open and slammed shut. Adder turned back to Kalil with his best seductive smile on his face. "Now. Where were we, my d—?"

He didn't get any further. Growling like a rabid dog, Kalil fisted both hands in Adder's hair and cut off his words with an aggressive kiss.

Chapter Six

For almost a month, Kalil had promised himself he wouldn't do this. Every morning when he woke up, every day when he tried not to stare at Adder during practice, every night when he jerked off to the hazy half-memory of Adder inside him, he'd sworn over and over that he was *not* going to give in to temptation. If he and Adder became lovers for real, it would fuck up everything. He couldn't risk it.

For twenty-seven days, he'd managed to stay strong. And now here he was, with his tongue in Adder's mouth and Adder's hands up the back of his shirt.

"Fuck you," Kalil breathed when Adder broke the kiss to bite his neck. "I can't believe—*shit,* God, do that again—can't *believe* you did this to me."

"My dearest K, you are the one who attacked *me*." Adder's tongue darted into Kalil's ear. He squeaked and yanked Adder's head back by the hair. Adder grinned. "Perhaps I should let Ms. Rivers coax me into bed. I think I like what jealousy does to you."

Kalil scowled. "I'm not jealous, asshole."

The grin widened, Adder's hazel eyes blazing with a combination of humor and lust which Kalil wished he didn't find so damn hot. "Of course not, darling." Dipping his head, Adder tongued the pulse point on Kalil's throat.

"I'm *not.*" Kalil arched his neck and pressed Adder's mouth harder against his skin. "Can you shut up about your enormous ego long enough to fuck me?"

Shaking his head, Adder slid both hands down the back of Kalil's jeans. "I'm on the bottom."

"I don't top."

"I don't either."

Unbelieving, Kalil grabbed Adder's arms and pushed him away, holding him at arm's length. "You do too, you fucking liar. You topped *me,* unless you lied about that."

"You were far too drunk to top. I was forced to."

"Yeah, well. I've seen you top other guys."

He got an arched brow in answer. "Oh? Do tell."

Kalil ground his teeth. "I caught you. Remember? When we shared a room in Greenville just before the Tabernacle gig and you brought that ridiculous little queen back with you? I walked in on you, you were pounding his ass so hard the headboard knocked a hole in the wall."

Adder's brows drew together in the stubborn expression Kalil had come to know and dread. "That was a girl."

"Well, 'she' had a pretty big dick for a girl."

"The sex change was still in process, you cretin."

Kalil sighed, wondering how weird it was to be this turned on right now. "Okay. Fine. So explain to me why you don't top."

"Why don't *you*?"

"I asked you first."

Adder flashed his unhinged grin, sending Kalil's hormones into overdrive and temporarily blotting out his irritation with the crazy green-haired bastard. "If I want to fuck someone, I'll go find a female. Which is, of course, the beauty of being bisexual. Honestly, what's the point in being with a man if you can't get a cock up your ass?"

Kalil thought about pointing out that *he* wasn't going to get a cock up *his* ass tonight, but let it drop. Adder would just point out that Kalil was gay and therefore was not sexually attracted to women, so his only opportunity of sticking his cock in anyone lay with the male of the species. Specifically, one particular male who was currently offering his own rear passage for Kalil's enjoyment.

Fucking shit, I'm thinking like him now. This cannot possibly be good.

Irritated and so turned on he couldn't see straight, Kalil grabbed Adder by his stupid orange and green paisley tie, pulled him across the room and shoved him onto the sofa. "Fine. Get your fucking clothes off."

To his relief, Adder seemed to have temporarily run out of teasing smiles and droll one-liners. He loosened the knot on the hideous tie, pulled it over his head and threw it on the floor. They both attacked Adder's black shirt at the same time. Kalil was pretty sure a couple of the buttons got torn off in the process of removing the shirt. He was also pretty sure he didn't give a shit. Hands clasping Adder's rib cage, he bent and dug his teeth into one pink nipple.

Adder's pained groan almost made up for Kalil's twenty-seven days of suffering all by itself. Long fingers wove into Kalil's hair. "Oooooh, gods. I could fall in love with your tongue."

Kalil, who had been working Adder's pants open, shoved a hand inside and pinched his hip to make him shut up. Adder hissed, but stopped talking, for which Kalil was grateful. The unexpected mention of falling in love—even though it was just with his tongue—made his stomach turn backflips.

It took a while to get Adder's pants off, partly because the satin stuck to his sweaty skin and partly because he was trying to take Kalil's shirt off at the same time. Eventually, though, Adder lay naked against the cushions, one leg thrown over the back of the sofa and both hands working to remove Kalil's jeans. Between the two of them, they managed to get Kalil's pants partway down. Kicking off his shoes, he squirmed out of the snug denim and pressed his body between Adder's spread thighs.

He couldn't help his sharp gasp when his erection aligned with Adder's. Grinning like the demon he was, Adder hooked a leg around Kalil's waist and thrust up. Kalil let out an embarrassing whine. "Jesus fucking Christ. Uh."

"Mmmm." Rearing up, Adder fastened his mouth to Kalil's neck and sucked so hard Kalil figured he'd see a blood blister there next time he looked in a mirror. "Fuck me, Special K."

Kalil shook loose of Adder's grip and sat back on his knees. He was about to shove a finger up Adder's butt when a thought struck him. "Goddammit."

"What?" Adder curled his fingers around his prick, not stroking, just holding on as if he was afraid it would fall off if he didn't.

"No rubbers. Hell, no lube either." Frustrated, Kalil raked a hand through his hair. "Shit."

"Use saliva, it works well enough."

"Yeah, for lube. But not for protection."

Adder quirked an eyebrow at him. "You wouldn't fuck me bare, darling?"

"Are you crazy? As much as you screw around? I don't think so."

If Adder was offended by that, he didn't let on. The tip of

his tongue came out to tease the corner of his mouth. “As it happens, I have a few condoms and packets of K-Y in my bag.”

Torn between relief and annoyance, Kalil gave Adder’s thigh a resounding smack. “Why the fuck didn’t you say so before?”

“I would have told you eventually. I simply wanted to see when you would notice the lack of proper supplies.” Adder let go of his cock, leaned sideways and rummaged through the yellow and teal flowered satchel beside the sofa. He emerged with a condom and a packet of lube, which he held out to Kalil. “Here you are, darling.”

Kalil shook his head. The condom was *orange*. Who used orange condoms?

He took it anyway. He’d cope with having a Day-Glo dick if it meant getting said appendage inside Adder sometime in the next two minutes.

Ripping the packet open, Kalil rolled the slick latex down over his cock. He snatched the lube from Adder’s palm and tore it open. Adder helpfully drew his legs up and apart to expose his rosy little hole. His hand shaking with eagerness and lust, Kalil squeezed some of the K-Y onto his fingers and slid two into Adder’s ass.

Adder moaned, eyelids fluttering and mouth falling open. “K. Yes.”

Gnawing his lower lip, Kalil pushed his fingers deeper and twisted, searching for Adder’s gland. His fingertip nudged a firm spot. Adder keened and clawed at the sofa. “Oh gods, oh. Oh. Please.”

Kalil swallowed a whimper. “You ready?” He left the “please be ready or I’m gonna come without ever getting inside you” unvoiced. What Adder didn’t know wouldn’t hurt him.

Adder nodded, breathing hard. “More than ready.”

Resisting the urge to shout “hallelujah”, Kalil spread the rest of the lube on his disturbingly colorful prick, scooted forward on his knees and poised the head of his cock at Adder’s hole. He grabbed hold of Adder’s hips and pushed. There was a second’s resistance, then his cock slid into Adder’s body.

They both groaned. Kalil shut his eyes and held still for a second, trying to gather the scattered shards of his control so he wouldn’t come right away and embarrass himself. *God,* Adder was tight, tighter than Kalil had expected, and so hot inside Kalil feared the condom might melt to his skin in permanent citrus-colored patches.

A hand caressed Kalil’s jaw. His eyes flew open. Adder was watching him with a sweet, solemn expression that made him feel like someone was tugging on his heart with a fishhook. He turned into the touch before he could give it too much thought, rubbing his cheek against Adder’s palm.

“My darling Kalil,” Adder purred. “If you don’t start moving *immediately*, I’ll be forced to leave you for my dildo.”

And just like that, the tender moment broke. Feeling strangely relieved, Kalil laughed. “Brat.”

Adder didn’t deny it. He wound his legs around Kalil’s waist and flexed, forcing him forward. Kalil let go of Adder’s hips just in time to catch himself with one hand on the back of the sofa and the other on one side of Adder’s head. The sudden movement drove Kalil’s prick deep into Adder’s butt.

The broken half-sob Adder let out made Kalil’s balls draw up and sweat bead on his upper lip. He pulled out and shoved back in, wondering if Adder would make that sound again.

He did, this time punctuating the sweet-hot noise with a bruising kiss and fingers digging painfully into Kalil’s back, and damned if that didn’t annihilate any intention Kalil had of making this last. Bracing his knees as best he could on the cushions, Kalil pounded into Adder's ass with all his strength.

"Fuck, yes," Adder growled, his lips still brushing Kalil's. "Harder. Gods."

Kalil wasn't sure "harder" was even possible, but he did his best to oblige. His hips snapped back and forth with enough force to make his teeth rattle. A particularly vicious thrust knocked Adder's head against the arm of the sofa. Kalil winced. "Sorry."

"'S okay. Didn't even feel it." Adder's legs tightened around Kalil's waist. "Come on, K. Fuck me hard. I won't break."

"I'm fucking you...as hard...as I can," Kalil panted. "Greedy bastard."

Adder flashed a feral grin. "Greedy for my Special K."

Something in Kalil's chest constricted in response to the possessive gleam in Adder's eyes. Adder referred to Kalil as his all the time, but this time felt different. Like he actually *meant* it. Kalil had no idea how to feel about that, never mind how to respond to it, so ignoring it altogether seemed like the best option.

Shifting his weight to his left elbow, Kalil curled his right hand around Adder's cock and started stroking. Adder made *that sound* again, and Kalil had to bite his lip to keep from coming. He'd make Adder come first or die trying.

"Yes, yes, yes," Adder murmured, glazed eyes half-shut and face damp with sweat. "K, gods, yes, so close."

Pushing up onto his knees, Kalil hammered Adder's ass in short, hard jabs, pulling on Adder's cock at the same time. Luckily, Kalil possessed a percussionist's coordination. "Come now. Come on."

Adder arched his back and wailed, semen spurting from his prick to coat his stomach and Kalil's fingers. Sheer surprise that Adder had actually come on command sent Kalil tumbling over the brink. He dug his fingers into Adder's thighs and hung on for dear life as the strongest orgasm he'd ever felt wrung all the sense out of him through his cock. He shook and cursed and kept thrusting until it ended, then collapsed onto Adder's chest.

They lay there in silence for a couple of minutes, both breathing hard. Adder's heartbeat galloped in Kalil's ear. Kalil smiled. He felt limp and spent and more relaxed than he'd been in ages. It wouldn't last, of course. But for now, he was happy to stay sprawled on top of Adder's naked body and pretend he hadn't just broken his number-one rule.

Eventually, Adder sighed and stretched. "Mmmm, that was magnificent."

"Totally." Kalil turned his head to lick a drop of sweat from Adder's sternum. The movement dislodged his soft cock from Adder's body. Kalil rolled up just enough to pull the condom off and throw it on the floor, then settled back onto Adder's body. "Okay, I think I just did all the moving I can do for now."

Adder laughed. The sound created a pleasant vibration against Kalil's cheek. "Then don't move, darling." Adder's arms wrapped around Kalil's back, fingers tracing a lazy trail up and down his spine. "You don't have any pressing engagements, do you?"

"No. You?"

"Not a thing." One arm tightened around Kalil's ribs. The other hand slid into his hair. "Stay here with me, sweetheart. My beautiful Kalil." Fingertips massaged Kalil's scalp in soothing circles. "Sleep for a while."

Kalil knew he ought not to. Later, when his brain started working again, he'd regret letting Adder lull him into this false sense of comfort. If he let himself fall asleep in Adder's arms, he'd never, *ever* be allowed to forget it. Adder would keep after him like a sexy, tattooed pit bull.

Too late to prevent that. You already fucked him.

He wasn't sure that really made him feel better, but he was way too tired to argue with himself about it. Tucking an arm around Adder's middle, he shut his eyes.

"Okay, this is the last time." Kalil zipped his jeans and faced Adder with the remains of his flagging determination. "The absolute *last* time."

On the bed, Adder rolled from his stomach to his back and grinned. "Whatever you say, darling."

"I mean it."

"Of course."

Grimacing, Kalil retrieved his shirt from the pile of clothes on the floor and pulled it on. Over the last ten days, Kalil had ended up in bed with Adder no less than five times. And every single time, he'd said the same thing—that it was the last time. That the two of them fucking was bad for both of them, bad for the band, and they absolutely, positively weren't doing it again.

At this point, he could hardly blame Adder for not believing him.

Ignoring Adder's smug smirk, Kalil plopped onto the edge of the bed to put his shoes on. "So, we're working on some new stuff at practice tomorrow, right?"

"Right. I want to make sure we have a good mix of older songs and new ones for the festival."

Kalil nodded. They had almost eight months before the

TART Festival, but he saw no reason to wait until the last minute to nail down a killer set. It was one point on which he and Adder agreed one hundred percent.

"I have some ideas for the rhythm section on 'Circling'." Kalil rose and raked the tangled hair out of his eyes. "I'd like to let y'all hear it, see what you think."

"Absolutely." Adder stretched like a panther and rolled onto his side. His cock flopped over, making the snake's tongue seem to flicker. "We should go to your place tomorrow night, if you're still dead set on pretending Harpo and Vi don't know about us. They'll both be home tomorrow night."

Kalil bent and fiddled with his shoelaces in a desperate bid to not ogle Adder's bare, sex-flushed body. "I told you, we're not doing this again."

"Yes. So you did." The mattress moved. Adder snagged Kalil's hair and tugged his head backward, so that he ended up staring into Adder's upside-down face. The smile on Adder's lips matched the one in his voice. "I'll see you tomorrow, lover."

Kalil let Adder kiss him, but broke the contact after a few seconds. He'd learned the hard way that if he got too involved in it, he'd end up staying for another round, and chances were high that he wouldn't leave. And he did *not* want that to happen. He was already dangerously close to seeing this thing between Adder and himself as a relationship. If he stayed the night with Adder, denying their connection would go from being merely difficult to being impossible.

"Yeah. See you." Shaking off Adder's grip, Kalil stood and headed for the door. He managed to resist looking back.

Chapter Seven

Adder liked to think of himself as a compassionate person. He gave of himself all the time. Money to the homeless, blood to the Red Cross, his music to the world. And there was nothing he wouldn't do for his friends. Vi and Harpo—and now Kalil—were more of a family to him than his parents and sister. Making them happy made *him* happy.

So why did his stomach turn excited somersaults when Kalil showed up on his doorstep nervously requesting a place to stay after a broken pipe flooded his apartment?

"I'm sorry," Kalil declared for at least the third time as he dropped his bags in the middle of the living room. "It shouldn't be but a couple of weeks. My landlord said they'd have the pipe fixed and the floors and drywall replaced by then."

Adder had his doubts about that, but he didn't want to voice them to Kalil, who already looked so mournful it broke Adder's heart. "My darling, our home is yours. You're welcome to stay as long as you need to."

The smile Kalil gave him made Adder's insides flutter. "Thanks, Adder. I really appreciate it." Shoving his hands into his back pockets, Kalil glanced around. "So. Um. I guess I'll sleep on the couch."

No one, least of all Adder, could possibly resist such an

opening. He sidled closer and ran a hand down Kalil's arm. "Don't sleep on the couch. Share my bed."

A very fetching blush colored Kalil's cheeks. "I...I don't—"

"Sweetheart, please." Adder slipped his arms around Kalil's shoulders and pulled him close. When Kalil didn't resist, Adder bent to nuzzle his soft ebony curls. "Vi and Harpo both know we're sleeping together."

"What?" Kalil wrestled out of Adder's embrace and stared at him, dark eyes wild. "I thought you were kidding about that before. How the hell do they know? Did you tell them?"

"I promised you I wouldn't."

"I know." Kalil glared. "Did you?"

The implication that he'd broken his promise hurt, but Adder knew better than to let it show. He lifted his chin and held Kalil's gaze. "No, Kalil, I did not."

"Then how do they know?"

"Hm, let me think." Adder touched a finger to his lips. "Because they're not completely blind?"

"Very funny." With a deep sigh, Kalil closed the distance between them, wrapped his arms around Adder's waist and pressed close. "Sorry. All this shit with my apartment's got me tense as hell."

The way Kalil slumped against his chest gave Adder a strange, warm feeling inside. He slid an arm around Kalil's ribs and buried the opposite hand in his hair. "It's all right, my sweet K," he whispered, rubbing Kalil's scalp in slow circles. "You've had a difficult day. It's understandable that you'd be stressed."

Kalil uttered a noncommittal hum and snuggled closer. Smiling, Adder rested his cheek on the top of Kalil's head. He loved the way Kalil melted every time Adder played with his hair.

"I guess I can share with you," Kalil mumbled into the hollow of Adder's throat. "But we'll have to work out some sort of system to let each other know if one of us has...company."

Adder's hand stilled at the back of Kalil's neck. "Yes, I suppose so." The words sounded casual in spite of the sudden tightness in Adder's throat. The thought of Kalil with someone else made his gut burn.

In fact, the thought of being with anyone but Kalil no longer seemed particularly appealing.

The realization frightened him. Every failed relationship he'd witnessed in the past had made him that much more determined never to fall prey to one himself. This thing with Kalil—whatever it was—had edged too close to relationship territory for comfort.

Not that Kalil wanted such a thing either. He'd made that abundantly clear. The stubborn ass had only recently given up on insisting he and Adder weren't lovers.

You need to get back on track, my dear. You've been so focused on conquering the enigmatic Mr. Sabatino that you simply haven't paid attention to anyone else. It's better for you both to see other people.

Adder curled his fingers in Kalil's wild locks and tugged. "Kiss me, darling."

Kalil laughed, but tilted his head for Adder's kiss anyway. Adder shut his eyes and sank into the feel of Kalil's soft, slick tongue against his. Expanding his circle of casual lovers didn't mean he had to give up sleeping with Kalil. His Special K would always have a place in his heart, and in his bed.

Footsteps shuffled across the floorboards to Adder's right, followed by the squeak of someone plopping onto the sofa. Kalil broke the kiss with a small distressed sound and pushed out of

Adder's arms. "Oh. Um. Vi. Didn't know you were home."

"Yep. I was in the kitchen trying to figure out what to make for dinner." Vi grinned from her spot on the couch. "Don't stop on my account. I was enjoying the show."

Kalil turned crimson. He hung his head so that his hair veiled his face and stared at the floor. "Uh. I already asked Adder, but is it okay with you and Harpo if I stay here for a while?"

"Fine by me." Rising to her knees, Vi turned and leaned over the back of the sofa. "Hey, Harpo!"

Harpo's voice floated down the hall, sounding faintly irritated. "What?"

"Kalil needs to stay with us for a while, that okay with you?"

A brief silence from Harpo's room was followed by Sheila's raised voice and Harpo shushing her. The door to Harpo's room opened. He strode into the living room stark naked except for Sheila's favorite fuchsia blouse tied around his waist. Adder stifled a laugh.

"You can totally stay with us, K." Harpo walked up to Kalil and slung an arm around his shoulders. "At least you and Adder can fuck now without having to make up excuses to be at each other's places."

Groaning, Kalil covered his face with his hands. "Shit."

Adder chuckled. He leaned close, putting his mouth beside Kalil's ear. "I told you, darling."

Adder wasn't a bit surprised when Kalil's building was condemned a week later due to multiple violations of building codes. The owner sold, the city scheduled the building for demolition and Kalil moved in on a more long-term basis.

The arrangement suited Adder just fine. Except for one little problem—living with Kalil made exclusivity with him far too easy. Days turned into weeks, and every gig found Adder ignoring multiple chances to bed various beautiful men and women in favor of going home with Kalil, fucking slow and sweet and falling asleep in each other's arms.

He didn't understand it at all. Sex with as many different partners as possible had been a staple of his life ever since Tammy and Terrence Noble had led him into the woods behind his high school and made him come until he saw supernovas behind his eyelids. Why, then, did he now feel so content with only one man?

It wasn't normal. Perhaps it was for others, but not for him. He had to break free of this terrifyingly comfortable inertia, or he'd lose himself for certain. All he needed was the motivation to act.

The fact that he eventually found it not within himself, but through Kalil, irked him to no end.

They were playing an all-night, multi-band Halloween show on a farm somewhere between Atlanta and LaGrange. The property belonged to a wealthy eccentric with a thing for pretty young people and earthy, visceral music.

It was Adder's favorite sort of gig—a hefty paycheck and an atmosphere thrumming with wild magic. He wove feathers into his hair, stripped to a brown suede thong and laid his soul bare to the revelers dancing by moonlight and firelight.

He was still hard when he and the band exited the stage after their set. His senses were hyper-aware, his brain buzzing. When he felt like this, all he wanted to do was fuck. With a man, with a woman, singly or in couples or in groups. It didn't matter.

Catching Kalil's eye, Adder shot him a feral grin. Kalil grinned back, brown eyes blazing, and Adder's cock jerked beneath the restraining suede. Maybe he could talk Kalil into a threesome tonight.

The four of them broke down the set and loaded the instruments into the van in record time. Adder could feel his bandmates' need almost as keenly as his own. The atmosphere of sensual freedom had gotten to all of them. Adder watched Harpo and Sheila dash hand in hand into one of the portable cabanas the property owner had thoughtfully provided, while Vi melted into the crowd with the two men who'd been staring at her all night. Kalil had wandered off into the trees behind the stage several minutes before.

Cupping his groin in one hand, Adder followed the path Kalil had taken. He needed to come, and he'd be damned if he would settle for his own hand when he could have Kalil's sinfully talented mouth.

What he saw stopped him in his tracks. Kalil—*his* Kalil—lounged against the trunk of a huge oak tree, both hands tucked behind his back, smiling while a man in a vampire costume leaned over him.

Adder knew that smile, that posture. Kalil was flirting. *Flirting.* With some idiot in a cape.

Growling under his breath, Adder stalked forward a few steps. And stopped. What the hell was he doing? He'd been looking for something to nudge him away from his growing intimacy with Kalil and back into familiar, comfortable, anonymous sex. If watching Kalil being seduced by a pathetic Goth basement dweller didn't qualify, nothing did.

Spinning on one bare heel, Adder strode back into the crowd. In a place like this, on a night like this one, he should have no trouble finding what he needed.

Sure enough, he hadn't been dancing for more than five minutes when a pair of hands skated down his back to cup his ass. A warm male body, bare-chested and just as aroused as Adder, molded itself to his back.

Humming with pleasure, Adder reached a hand behind him and tangled his fingers into a head of thick hair nearly level with his. He laughed. It wasn't often he hooked up with someone as tall as himself.

"Why, hello there," he purred, rubbing his backside against the stranger's obvious erection.

"Hi." The sharp chin digging into his shoulder shifted. Warm lips planted a wet kiss behind his ear. "You're gorgeous."

"Thank you." Adder dropped his head forward so the man could kiss and lick the back of his neck. "I wish I could say the same, but I haven't seen you yet." Letting go of the man's hair, Adder slid his hand down and backward to grab a palmful of what felt like a skirt. "I do like the way you feel, though."

The stranger stepped back with a chuckle. "Turn around and look, then."

Adder did, and it was all he could do not to whimper like a little girl. The man standing not a foot away from him was an absolute vision of virile male beauty. Long, dark hair curling around muscular shoulders, strong jaw, a wide mouth tailor-made for doing wicked things in the dark. Brown eyes with a gaze direct enough to make Adder feel flayed raw. Wide shoulders, muscled chest, a flat belly with an enviable six-pack. And gods, the man was wearing a kilt. A red and black kilt that hung low enough to show the tops of his hipbones.

Adder smiled. "Mmmm. I do love a man in a kilt."

"And I love a man in next to nothing." The man raked a hungry gaze up and down Adder's sweat-covered body. "Adder, right? I saw you play. You're fantastic."

"Thank you very much." Adder stepped closer and laid a palm on the stranger's chest. "And what shall I call you, handsome?"

The lovely lips curved into a smile. "You can call me anything you want."

Adder laughed. "I believe I've had enough of dancing for the night. What say we retire to the barn for a bit?"

In answer, Highlander—as Adder had already dubbed the man in his head—clamped a hand onto Adder's wrist and dragged him through the sea of people toward the old wooden structure crouching on the outskirts of the field. Adder let himself be led, ignoring the not entirely pleasant way his stomach fluttered. So what if Highlander's hair was just a little too long, his skin too pale, his eyes not quite the right shade of brown? After so long with one person, Adder was out of practice in having sex with multiple partners. That was why he didn't feel as comfortable as he should have. He just had to get used to it again.

The barn obviously hadn't housed livestock in a while. It smelled dry and musty, with only a faint animal odor beneath the scent of old hay. Adder shivered and rubbed his arms. The night was unseasonably warm, but it was chilly away from the bonfires and body heat. With any luck, Highlander would warm him up.

Speaking of which... Adder glanced around, a smile on his lips. Moans and grunts and the slap of bare skin on bare skin floated from a couple of the stalls, and the boards of the hay loft overhead creaked with what sounded like a veritable orgy. The presence of other couples and groups didn't bother Adder. A dark barn with unseen strangers fucking in the corners was far more private than some of the places he'd had sex in the past.

Pulling him into one of the stalls, Highlander slammed Adder against the rough boards and took his mouth in an aggressive kiss. Adder closed his eyes, opened his mouth and reminded the herd of wildebeests trampling through his stomach that he wanted this. He could feel Highlander's cock against his hip, hard and huge. What self-respecting bottom wouldn't want that inside him? Of course he wanted it.

A big hand tugged his thong aside, grabbed his testicles and squeezed to the point of pain. He yelped, the sound muffled by Highlander's tongue. The pressure let up instantly. Fingers inched behind his balls, caressing his perineum in soft, gentle strokes. He moaned and squirmed away.

No, that was wrong. He wasn't trying to get *away*. What a strange thing to think. He was trying to get *closer*.

"Yes, that's it," he whispered into Highlander's mouth.

Highlander laughed, the sound low and rough. "Like that, do you?"

Adder wasn't about to admit he'd been talking to himself. He managed a smile. "Mmmm, yes."

"Good." With one last sharp nip to Adder's bottom lip, Highlander drew his hand out of Adder's thong and turned him to face the wall. "Wanna fuck you."

Adder's heart lurched. Swallowing a sudden rush of bile in his throat, he hooked his thumbs into his thong, shoved it down and pulled it off before he could change his mind. He needed this. Needed the thrill of a new cock inside him. He was just a little nervous, because it had been so long. It would pass.

Wouldn't it?

Behind him, Adder heard the clink of a buckle and the buzz of a zipper, followed by a muffled thump which he assumed was the kilt hitting the wood-plank floor. He stared at a knothole in the wall inches from his face and listened to the sound of a condom packet being ripped open. He didn't dare look over his shoulder the way he would've done if it had been Kalil about to fuck him. For some reason, the thought of seeing Highlander's face right now made him feel sick.

Hands locked onto Adder's hips, thumbs spreading his ass cheeks. Sweat broke out on his brow as a thick finger traced the whorl of his anus. His pulse raced and his hands shook. From excitement, most likely. It didn't matter that he'd never reacted this way before. There was a first time for everything.

The finger pushed and slipped inside, and Adder knew, in a blinding burst of insight, that this was wrong. This wasn't what he wanted. Wasn't *who* he wanted.

Hell and damnation.

Battling panic, Adder reached back to grab Highlander's wrist. "Wait."

"What?" The finger withdrew, the hand moving to pet Adder's hip. "I'm not hurting you, am I?"

"No, it's just...I..." Adder bit his lip against the tremor in his voice.

"You what?" Strong arms pulled Adder to the big, warm body behind him. Highlander's sheathed cock rubbed between his buttocks, teasing his hole. "Please tell me you're not a virgin. You can't take me if you are."

Adder fought a wild urge to laugh. It had been years since anyone had mistaken him for a virgin.

Gathering his courage, Adder wriggled around to face Highlander. If he was going to send the man away *now*, of all times, he could at least have the guts to look him in the eye.

Adder opened his mouth to speak, but the words died on his lips when he got a glimpse over Highlander's broad shoulder at the very familiar form standing in the stall doorway.

Kalil.

Oh, gods.

Chapter Eight

Kalil knew he should leave. Just turn around and head back into the crowd. But Adder's wide eyes stared straight into his, and he couldn't move. Couldn't speak. Couldn't even fucking *breathe.*

It wasn't like he'd never seen Adder with anyone else. He had. More than once. But not in the last few weeks. In fact, more than two months had passed—that he knew of, anyway—since Adder had hooked up with anyone but him. That was an eternity in Adder time.

Without even realizing it, he'd gotten used to having Adder to himself. And now there the bastard was, naked and being pawed by some brainless musclehead.

Kalil didn't want to think about why that *hurt* like it did.

While Kalil stood with his feet glued to the floor, Adder murmured to the walking piece of meat and pushed on his chest. The guy stumbled back a bit, and Kalil couldn't hold back a snicker.

The stranger whirled around. His heavy brows drew together when he spotted Kalil. "What the hell, man? This is private."

Kalil laughed out loud, in spite of the gnawing pain in his chest. Nobody, no matter how good-looking he was, could pull off the naked-except-for-boots-and-a-condom look with any degree of success.

“Sorry to interrupt,” he lied. “I was looking for Adder. I guess I found him.”

The guy glowered. “Yeah, well, we were kind of busy, so if you don’t mind...”

Musclehead turned his back to Kalil and slid a pair of bulky arms around Adder’s waist. Kalil managed to stifle the urge to run at the jackass and start punching. Mr. Steroid probably wouldn’t even notice, and how embarrassing would *that* be?

“Actually, I...I changed my mind.”

Adder’s voice shook in a way Kalil had never heard before. Alarmed, he strode forward, pulled Musclehead backward by one beefy arm and grasped Adder’s shoulders. He ignored the stranger’s indignant exclamation and concentrated on Adder. “Hey, are you okay?”

Adder nodded, but his smile looked anemic and his face was ghost-white in the gloom. “Fine, I’m fine. Yes.”

“This guy didn’t—”

“No,” Adder and Musclehead protested at the same time. Adder shot the man an apologetic look over Kalil’s shoulder. “No, I came here with him willingly. I just...changed my mind. That’s all.”

Behind Kalil, Musclehead growled. “Great. Just great.” There was a rubbery snap, then the sound of one very pissed-off man getting dressed. “Cock tease.”

Adder winced and chewed his lip as booted feet stomped across the stall, through the barn and out. “Oh my.”

“Yeah, ‘oh my’. You’re lucky that asshole didn’t hit you or anything.” Kalil reached up to touch Adder’s cheek. “Are you sure he didn’t...you know. *Do* anything to you? You seem kind of shook up."

"I promise he didn't." Adder shrugged. "I simply decided I didn't want him to fuck me after all."

"Why not?" *And why the hell are you asking that, dumbass?* Kalil had no idea, other than sheer curiosity. Adder wasn't usually one to turn down a chance for a fuck.

"Did you see the man's cock? It was *huge.*" Adder tossed a lock of hair out of his eyes, dislodging a couple of feathers in the process. "Slut though I am, I have no desire to be split in half."

He's lying, Kalil realized as Adder's gaze slid sideways. *And upset about it.*

In the short time they'd known each other, Kalil had learned that Adder could stare a person straight in the eye and spin the most outrageous lies with a sincerity which made the most hardcore skeptics believe every word. The only times Kalil had ever known Adder to break eye contact was when he felt deeply troubled by something and wanted to hide it.

Worried, Kalil stared into Adder's face, trying to read his expression in the faint light from the window. "You sure you're okay?"

"Yes, dammit!" Adder pushed Kalil's hand away and stepped out of reach. "Stop it."

Stung, Kalil crossed his arms and scowled. "Fine. You don't have to be such a fucking jackass about it."

"Well, you're treating me like a child."

"I was *worried* about you, asshole."

"Yes, well, thanks *awfully,* but I think I can handle myself just fine."

Kalil blew out a frustrated breath. "Shit. Excuse the hell out of me for wanting to make sure that steroid-poisoned fuck wasn't hurting you."

Adder looked up, his expression hidden by darkness. "I don't need you to *rescue* me."

Angry, a little hurt and a lot confused, Kalil turned away and strode across the small space to the half-open door. "Fine. I'm going home. You can hitchhike since you handle yourself so fucking well."

Adder's hand on his arm stopped him. "What about Vi and Harpo?"

"Harpo's going to Sheila's tonight. Vi's catching a ride later with some friends. I'm taking the van. That's why I was trying to find you, to see if you were staying or if you wanted to..." *To come home with me. To spend the rest of the night and all the next day in bed.* Kalil wasn't about to say any such thing *now.* He shook off Adder's grip. "See you whenever."

This time, he made it almost to the barn door before Adder caught him. The bastard spun him around so fast he almost fell and fisted one hand in his hair. "Who was that man I saw you with earlier? The vampire?"

"Somebody I know." Kalil squirmed, but couldn't get away from Adder's iron grip. "Let go, dammit."

The fingers in his hair tightened. Adder's other hand clamped onto Kalil's upper arm so hard he winced. "Who was he, Kalil? Are you fucking him?"

Sheer surprise stopped Kalil's struggling. He stared at Adder with his jaw hanging open. "How is that any of your goddamn business?" Kalil demanded when he recovered enough to speak. "You came in here with some guy whose name I bet you don't even know so he could fuck you, and you're standing there, *naked,* grilling me about who I've been talking to?" He grabbed both of Adder's wrists and twisted hard, forcing Adder's fingers to loosen and let go. "Fuck you."

Adder stood still as a post, his eyes in shadow and his bare skin gleaming in the moonlight. "I don't like seeing you with someone else."

Kalil's heart gave a peculiar twist. Not knowing what to say or how to react, Kalil looked away. "Yeah, well, that's too bad. I'm not your boyfriend." *And I don't want to be. Not at all. Not even a little.*

He wondered how many times he'd have to tell himself that before he believed it.

A soft, pained noise was the only warning Kalil got before Adder pounced. Kalil's back hit the ground so hard he actually saw stars for a second. When his vision cleared, the first thing he saw was Adder's fist flying toward his face. He grabbed it in midair and shoved, sending Adder sprawling in the dirt. Kalil rolled, straddled the other man and pinned his wrists above his head.

"What the fuck do you think you're doing?" Kalil shouted. "Have you finally lost what little sanity you had?"

"Get. *Off.*" Adder's hips bucked upward.

Kalil dug his knees into Adder's sides and hung on. "Calm the fuck down, then."

Adder stared into his eyes, panting. Kalil saw something like desperation flow over Adder's features. The worry he'd felt before came creeping back. "Adder, look—"

Before Kalil could figure what exactly he wanted to say, Adder reared up and kissed him hard.

Taken by surprise, Kalil let go of Adder's wrists. Adder sat up and crushed Kalil against him, forcing Kalil's mouth open with his tongue. With a mental shrug, Kalil wrapped arms and legs around Adder's nude body and kissed back with enthusiasm.

It was a relief, in a way. Kalil still had no clue what bug had crawled up Adder's ass tonight, but what the hell. Maybe a little angry sex would give them both enough distance from the whole mess that they could ignore it later without it being too weird.

One of Adder's hands unclenched from Kalil's butt and wormed between their bodies to fumble with his button fly. Kalil helped him, and together they managed to get the jeans undone without breaking the kiss. Adder's long fingers fished out Kalil's cock and curled around the shaft.

The touch sent sparks shooting up Kalil's spine. He squirmed until he could get hold of Adder's prick, grabbed it and started stroking. The angle wasn't ideal, but Kalil didn't care. He was hard as a rock, his whole body pulsing with the need for release. No one but Adder had ever been able to take Kalil's lust level from zero to sixty in less than a minute.

Moaning, Kalil rocked his hips as much as he could without knocking them both over. His wrist was starting to cramp, but Adder was making those sweet whimpering noises, his hand had begun to spasm around Kalil's prick and *God,* Kalil was going to fucking explode if he didn't come soon.

Just as Kalil felt the telltale tingle in his thighs, Adder tore his mouth from Kalil's and stared straight into his eyes. Kalil came with his gaze locked to Adder's and Adder's semen spurting across his hand.

Kalil slumped against Adder's chest, partly because he felt limp as a rag in the wake of his orgasm, but mostly so he wouldn't have to see the open, unguarded expression on Adder's face. That look gave Kalil a strange, tight feeling in the pit of his stomach, and he didn't want to examine it too closely.

They sat there for a while with their arms around each other, breathing hard. Adder petted Kalil's back and ran gentle fingers through his hair. It felt good. Kalil hummed in content. He nuzzled Adder's neck. Adder smelled like sweat, bonfire smoke and a whiff of spicy cologne. The cologne must've belonged to Musclehead, because Adder never wore the stuff.

The memory of Adder being molested by that goddamn caveman sent a hot surge of anger—jealousy maybe?—through Kalil's blood. He scrunched his nose. He didn't like that any more than he liked the way Adder could melt him with nothing more than a thumb rubbing the back of his neck.

"Who was he, K?" Adder murmured after a few silent minutes.

"How should I know? You're the one he was groping, not me." Kalil knew he sounded petulant, but he didn't care. What the hell kind of guessing game did Adder think he was playing here?

Adder breathed a quiet laugh into Kalil's hair. "Not him, darling. The man *you* were with. The vampire."

"Oh. Just somebody I knew from high school. We went out a few times, but it never did go anywhere." Remembering what Adder had said earlier, Kalil smiled and shook his head. "I'm not fucking him. We were just catching up."

"Mmmm." Adder's fingers traced up and down Kalil's spine. "But you followed him into the woods."

"No, I went behind a tree to take a piss and we spotted each other when I was heading back toward the backstage area." *And why does it matter so much to you, anyway?* Kalil didn't voice that question. He figured he might not want to hear the answer.

Adder shifted and drew back. He was smiling, relief clear as day in his eyes. "Pissing in the woods, darling? How very primitive of you."

"Yeah, well, have you *seen* the Port O Lets they have here? Totally gross."

They fell silent. Adder studied Kalil's face with disturbing intensity. Kalil fidgeted and looked away.

With a soft sigh, Adder tilted his head and pressed a light kiss to Kalil's lips. "Well. What say we go home now, my sweet? I'm freezing, and I'd quite like to warm up in bed, with you."

Kalil glanced up. The teasing light was back in Adder's eyes. He winked, and Kalil laughed. He wiped his sticky palm on his jeans, planted his hands on Adder's shoulders for balance and heaved himself to his feet. "You wouldn't be cold if you had clothes on, you know."

"Yes, but too many clothes just get in my way on stage." Adder took the hand Kalil held down to him and let Kalil pull him off the ground. He cleaned the spunk off his hand using Kalil's already-soiled T-shirt. "Besides, you *know* what an exhibitionist I am, darling."

"No kidding." Kalil glanced around while he tucked his prick back into his jeans and buttoned up. "Did you come in here naked or did you leave that thong someplace?"

"It's back in the stall. One moment, I'll get it." Adder gave Kalil a knowing look over his shoulder as he strode toward the stall. "I wouldn't want to embarrass you by walking outside naked."

"Uh-huh. More like you don't want to lose your favorite thong." Kalil glared at a girl peeking from around the doorway of another stall. She popped out of sight just as Adder emerged again with the bit of dirty suede in his hand. "God, that thing's filthy."

"Indeed." Grinning, Adder pulled on the thong. "But then again, so am I." He wiggled his butt.

Kalil laughed and gave Adder's bare ass a smack. "Shut up and let's go."

They were out the door and halfway across the field to the

artists' parking area when it struck Kalil that they were holding hands. Just strolling through the October night with their fingers laced together. Like *boyfriends* or something.

That's not what we are. Is it?

Kalil stole a glance at Adder. Adder met his gaze with a sweet smile and squeezed Kalil's hand.

Huh. Maybe we are.

For the first time, Kalil thought maybe that wouldn't be such a bad thing after all.

"Kalil!" Adder flung open the bedroom door. "Aren't you ready yet? Jordan's expecting us in twenty minutes, we need to go."

"I'm almost ready." Kalil yanked his pants up as fast as he could without catching his balls in the open zipper. "Shut the door, would you?"

"Oh, are you afraid Harpo or Vi will see you in your underwear?" Leaving the door open, Adder stalked across the floor, wrapped both arms around Kalil's waist and kissed the end of his nose. "My poor shy darling."

Kalil laughed. "We can't all be closet strippers like you."

"My dear Special K, I've never been a closet *anything.*" Adder drew back when Kalil nudged him. "I'm going to check on Harpo. If he's still on the phone with Sheila he might need rescuing."

"Okay. I'll be out in a sec."

Adder gave Kalil a quick peck on the lips, then turned and strolled out into the hall. "Hurry, sweetheart."

Kalil gazed after him with a smile. When he thought about it, Kalil couldn't pinpoint exactly what had changed in the ten days since Halloween. He and Adder hadn't suddenly started making moon-eyes at each other or calling one another pet names. Well, Adder did, but he did that with everyone and always had. Neither of them had made any official claim on the other. But things were definitely different. They were a couple now. They both knew it, even if neither of them had ever acknowledged that fact out loud.

After all the angst he'd gone through trying to avoid being in a relationship with Adder, it was kind of a relief to just let it happen the way it had wanted to ever since their first meeting. He was bound and goddamn determined to enjoy it while it lasted.

Grabbing his shirt from the bed, Kalil shrugged it on. He pulled on his shoes and hurried into the living room, buttoning his shirt as he went. "All right, I'm ready."

Vi jumped up from her perch on the arm of a chair, twisting her hands together. "God, I'm nervous."

Adder slipped an arm around Vi's shoulders. "Don't be nervous, love. I'm sure whatever it is Jordan wants to talk to us about, it's something good." He kissed the top of her head, gave her a squeeze and let her go. "Harpo! Come *on*, we're going to be late."

"Yeah, yeah, I'm coming." Harpo jogged down the hall and into the living room, stuffing his cell phone in the pocket of his pinstriped jacket. "Since when do you care if we're a few minutes late anyway?"

"Since we have a professional relationship with Jordan Rivers." Adder lifted his satchel from the floor beside the sofa and slung it over his shoulder. "Come along, children. I'll drive."

Shaking his head, Kalil held out his hand. "Give me the

keys, Adder."

"Darling, please. I'm perfectly capable of getting us there safely."

"Adder. Your license is suspended, remember?"

"But—"

"Give 'em."

Adder glared. Kalil wiggled his fingers. With a put-upon sigh, Adder dug the van's keys out of his pocket and dropped them into Kalil's hand. "You're a hard man, Kalil."

"You know what they say," Vi piped up as she followed Harpo out the apartment door. "A hard man is good to find."

Adder's pout morphed into a salacious smile. "Oh yes. He certainly is." He wound an arm around Kalil's shoulders and nuzzled his hair.

Kalil's chest went tight. That appeared to be happening more and more lately. He tilted his face up and kissed Adder's chin to cover the weird mix of discomfort and giddiness inside him. He slipped his arm around Adder's waist, and they left the apartment.

Driving through the Atlanta streets to Jordan's office, Kalil used the heavy traffic as an excuse to avoid talking while his bandmates speculated about why Jordan had asked them to meet with her this afternoon. He wished he could shake off his lingering unease about his relationship with Adder. It seemed like the harder he tried to ignore it, the more it prodded at him.

He wasn't even sure why, really. He wanted Adder. More than he'd ever wanted anybody. And it wasn't just sex. Musically, Adder was worlds above anyone else Kalil had ever known. Besides that, he liked being with Adder. Liked his sharp, dry humor, his intelligence, even his weird clothes and penchant for melodramatics. So why, Kalil wondered, did he still feel like he was waiting for the other shoe to drop?

Because maybe the sensible parts of you realize how it's gonna eventually end, when he gets tired of you.

Kalil scowled. He tried not to think about what would happen to him when Adder eventually—inevitably—broke up with him, but he couldn't help it. Maybe he and Adder could put aside any hard feelings from a failed relationship. But if they couldn't, Kalil knew sure as shit which of them would be leaving the band.

The thought made him want to throw up. He'd found his musical soul mates in these three people. The need to keep that creative connection in his life was almost a physical ache.

The thing was, the idea of living without Adder's half-sweet, half-evil smile scared him even more than the thought of losing the band. And he had no idea how to deal with that.

A sharp tug on his hair brought him out of his thoughts. He gave Vi an irritated look in the rearview mirror. "What the hell, Vi?"

"Oh, sorry to disturb your daydream, but you missed the turn." She smacked his shoulder. "Pay attention, dumbass."

"Fucking goddamn shit." He jerked the wheel sideways, narrowly missing a black Mustang, and swerved around the next right-hand turn amid the blaring of multiple horns. "Sorry. I'll make the block and park across the street."

"Perhaps you should have let me drive after all," Adder declared.

Kalil shot him a barbed glare. "There's a reason you got five reckless driving tickets in as many months, you know."

Adder started to speak, then closed his mouth and gave Kalil a narrow look. Kalil peered out the windshield at the bumper-to-bumper traffic, ignoring Adder's skull-penetrating stare. Maybe if he didn't make eye contact, Adder would get the hint and leave him the hell alone. Kalil did *not* want to discuss his stupid fears with Adder, or anyone else. Certainly not now, and preferably not ever.

The last few minutes of the drive passed in silence. Kalil found an empty spot on the street half a block from the building housing Rivers Productions. The four of them walked up the sidewalk, crossed the street, entered the building and climbed the stairs to the loft without saying a word.

Kalil felt Adder's gaze like an itch on the back of his neck the whole time. He stifled a sigh. Quiet, intense Adder usually meant a grilling later.

Oh well. He could always distract the stubborn bastard with sex. Adder may be more mercurial than an old thermometer, but he was reliably horny.

The blue-haired secretary whose name Kalil could never remember wasn't there. Jordan stepped out of her office and greeted them with a huge smile. "Hello, dears! Come in, come in. Would anyone like some tea? Or a soda?"

They glanced at each other. "No, thank you," Adder answered. "I think we're all quite anxious to find out what you wanted to discuss with us."

"And I'm anxious to tell you." Crossing the room, she hooked her arm through Adder's and led him toward her office. "Let's sit down and talk. I think you'll all be very excited by my news."

Kalil, Harpo and Vi trailed behind Adder and Jordan. Kalil tried to squash the automatic swell of jealousy when Adder turned his most dazzling smile to Jordan. The woman could make or break their careers. Of course Adder was going to keep flirting with her. He didn't *need* to, but Kalil knew he wouldn't stop. He couldn't seem to help himself. Not that knowing that made it any easier to watch.

Adder drew away from Jordan and took Kalil's hand as they filed into the office. Kalil gave what he hoped was a relaxed smile. The last thing in the world he wanted was for Adder to realize how much his flirting with Jordan bothered Kalil. Either Kalil would come across as needy and clingy, or Adder would flirt twice as hard just to watch Kalil seethe. Neither option was particularly appealing.

Adder's expression said he knew damn well something was bothering Kalil, but he didn't say anything. Instead, he laced his fingers through Kalil's and faced Jordan again. "So, Jordan, my love. What's this exciting news you have?"

She sat and rested her forearms on her desk. "What would the four of you say to a national tour before the TART Festival?"

Harpo's mouth fell open. "Are you serious?"

"Very." Jordan's keen gaze met each of theirs in turn, lingering on Adder's face. "In the past few weeks, I've traveled all over the country promoting this festival. I've been playing music by the bands I've signed so far for TART. And everywhere I go, people want to know who you are and how to get in touch with you." She grinned. "I've spoken with at least a dozen club managers who are falling all over themselves to book you. If you kids are up for it, I can set you up a month or more of club dates right now."

Oh my God. A national tour? Kalil glanced around. Harpo and Vi wore the same stunned expressions Kalil felt on his own face. Even Adder seemed surprised, and the man was a master at hiding his reactions.

"It's great that people are interested in us," Kalil said, breaking the silence. "There's no need for you to do all that extra work, though. I'm sure we can handle our own booking."

Jordan gave him a look which suggested she knew he was

concerned with other things than her workload. "Probably. But there's a lot involved in setting up a tour. It's different from just playing gigs within driving distance of Atlanta two or three times a week. I can help you with that."

Four pairs of eyes swiveled to Adder. Kalil stifled a laugh. All of them—him included—looked to Adder as the leader, the decision maker, even though he never actually made a decision without knowing they all agreed on it.

If Adder noticed the sudden attention, he didn't let on. Maybe he was used to it.

"Your help would be greatly appreciated," Adder said. His fingers clenched and unclenched around Kalil's, the only outward sign of how hard he was thinking. "My question is, why would you offer us such help?" He leaned forward a little, his expression earnest. "Please don't take that the wrong way, Jordan. It's just that Kalil is perfectly correct that it's a lot of extra work for you, on top of an already overloaded schedule. Why would you do that?"

Listening to the tiny thread of apprehension in Adder's voice, Kalil thought he knew what Adder was thinking. The nut actually believed Jordan would book and manage their tour in exchange for sexual favors from him. Ridiculous, of course, but Adder's brain just didn't work like a normal person's.

That fact that Adder clearly didn't want to provide any favors made Kalil feel warm and sort of smug.

Jordan clasped her hands together. "I'd do it because you guys are going to hit it big. You're going to be *huge*. And I'd really like a piece of that."

Vi's face lit up. "You mean you want to be our manager?"

"I do. Very much." Jordan glanced at each of them in turn. "You don't have to answer right now, if you'd rather not. Think about it, and let me know. If you decide you'd rather have someone else, or to keep managing yourselves, no hard feelings. I'll give you contact info for clubs in several cities. But I think I have a great deal to offer you as a manager, and I know you all have a lot to offer *me* in terms of profit."

The four of them looked at each other. Adder studied Vi's and Harpo's faces. Kalil could read their agreement in their expressions. When Adder turned to him, a question in those big hazel eyes, Kalil smiled and nodded. They needed a manager, and he knew—his irrational jealousy notwithstanding—that Jordan was the woman for the job.

The decision made, Adder let go of Kalil's hand and reached across the desk. "Jordan, I do believe you're hired."

Beaming, she took his hand and shook. "Excellent. I can't wait to make you kids as rich and famous as you deserve."

Kalil didn't miss the way Jordan's fingers caressed Adder's palm as they pulled apart. He swallowed the growl that wanted to come out. Acting like a caveman just because she was caressing the hand that had jerked him off that morning was childish. Adder flirted with her, sure, but he flirted with everyone. It was his way of interacting with the world. Kalil knew for a solid fact that he was the only one who shared Adder's bed these days.

The knowledge made Kalil feel as if a tiny sun had taken up residence in his solar plexus. And just how fucking scary was that?

Chapter Nine

Kalil had been moody and out of sorts all day. Adder had noticed, naturally. Dear, sweet Special K didn't hide his emotions nearly as well as he believed he did, and Adder was an unusually observant person. Especially when it came to his lovers.

Not that one needed to be all that observant to see that something was bothering Kalil. Even the most oblivious person could have read Kalil's turmoil in the crease between those big, beautiful eyes.

That night, after Kalil almost fucked the life out of him, Adder decided he needed to bite the proverbial bullet and ask Kalil what was wrong. Rough sex was one thing—and a very *good* thing, in Adder's opinion—but there was rough and then there was *rough.* A bruised and tender ass was only sexy in stories.

Adder rolled over and gathered Kalil into his arms before the stubborn thing could recover enough to fight him. "What's wrong, darling?"

Kalil blinked glazed eyes. "Huh? What're you talking about?"

"Kalil, my dear, you've been brooding all day." Adder kissed Kalil's sweaty brow. "What is it, love? Is it Jordan? You know I'm not sleeping with her, nor do I plan to."

That hit a nerve, judging by the way Kalil grimaced. "No, I know that." He looked away. "Doesn't matter anyway."

It did, and they both knew it, but Adder didn't bother pointing out the obvious. He stroked the damp hair away from Kalil's face. "Something's bothering you," he whispered, burying his hand in Kalil's curls. "I wish you'd tell me what it is."

Kalil's breathing faltered for a moment. His fingers dug into Adder's ribs. "You'll think it's stupid."

"I promise I won't." Adder slung one bare leg over Kalil's hips. "Tell me, darling."

Sighing, Kalil tucked his head beneath Adder's chin. *So he won't have to look me in the eye,* Adder thought, but didn't say it. He held his tongue and waited.

"What's your name?" Kalil asked after a long silence.

Of all the things Adder might have expected to hear, that wasn't one of them. He frowned. "You know my name. It's Adder."

"Yeah, I know, but..." Kalil shifted in Adder's embrace. His palm slid down Adder's side to curl around his thigh. "You know so much about me, Adder. You know where I grew up, where I went to school, that I'm dyslexic. You've even met my family and seen my baby pictures. But I don't know a damn thing about you. Not even your real name."

Adder worried his lower lip between his teeth. He thought he knew where this was going. Kalil evidently felt his life was an open book, whereas Adder's was a locked vault of mysteries, and he wished to balance the scales before baring himself any further. It was understandable. Adder probably would have wanted the same thing had their situations been reversed.

That didn't make it any easier to talk about himself, however. He guarded his secrets fiercely, even the ones that didn't matter, simply because they were *his*. In spite of his exhibitionist tendencies, in spite of his constant craving for attention, he liked to have total control over what people knew about him.

Kalil wasn't just "people", though. He was a bandmate. A lover. A friend. The closest thing to a real relationship Adder had ever found.

He's mine, Adder admitted to himself, finally. *We belong to each other, for now at least, and he deserves to know me.*

"I was born Adirondack Rain Madison," Adder said, his thumb rubbing circles behind Kalil's ear. "My sister used to call me Adder for short. When she learned what an adder actually was, she said it was appropriate because I was mean as a snake."

"You're not mean. Crazy, but not mean." Kalil's arm cinched around Adder's waist. "So you got the tattoo to go with the nickname, I guess."

"Yes, I did. And I had my name legally changed to Adder as an homage to the tattoo which launched my career. Well, in a way."

Kalil chuckled. "Okay, you can't say that and not explain it."

"Well, then. Explain I shall." Adder massaged Kalil's scalp, just to hear the soft little hum Kalil let out whenever he did that. "I designed the tattoo myself, and had the work done when I was sixteen."

"Sixteen? I thought they weren't allowed to do a tat unless you're at least eighteen."

"Yes, that's true. But my roommate at the time had an aunt who was a tattoo artist. She was an incredible artist, and I desperately wanted her to do my tattoo, but I had no money to pay her, and I certainly couldn't go to an artist who might notice that the I.D. I had was fake, and therefore refuse to work on me. So Corinne agreed to tattoo me for free in exchange for me modeling the piece at a tattoo convention. Her shop wasn't well established yet, and she was looking to build her clientele."

Kalil lifted his head to give Adder an incredulous look. "But you were underage. And *naked.* In *public.* Didn't she get in trouble?"

"No. No one questioned my age. Corinne said it was probably because I had an air of maturity." The memory of all those strangers admiring his nude body still had the power to make Adder shiver. Gods, he loved that feeling. "Anyway, a local fashion designer spotted me and decided I would be the perfect model for his new clothing line. That was my second paying job, and I made far more at that than I did mopping floors and scrubbing toilets at Breakfast Barn."

Kalil was staring at Adder as if he'd never really seen him before. "I never knew you were a model."

"It was only for a year or so, but Josiah paid me extremely well. I was able to save enough money to tide me over while I began building my reputation as a musician." Adder smiled, remembering his former employer. The man had taught him so much, both in and out of bed. "Modeling for Josiah allowed me to keep myself fed, clothed and sheltered while pursuing my dream of being a professional musician. So you see, if it weren't for that tattoo, Josiah wouldn't have found me, and I might not be where I am today."

Lifting his hand, Kalil traced the line of Adder's jaw with one fingertip. "When did you leave home?"

It didn't surprise Adder in the least that Kalil had made that particular deduction. Kalil was smart and clever, and Adder had certainly dropped enough clues. "On my fifteenth birthday."

"Why did you leave?" Kalil's eyes narrowed. "Your

parents—"

"Were perfectly adequate, if somewhat overprotective," Adder interrupted. "I wasn't mistreated, simply misunderstood and somewhat stifled." He shrugged. "I wanted to be a star, and I did not want to wait until I was an adult to begin working toward that goal. Home life and school got in the way. So I left."

A wan smile curved Kalil's kiss-bruised lips. "You're something else, you know that?"

"Yes, actually, I do." Catching Kalil's hand in his, Adder kissed the warm palm. "Now you know things about me even Harpo and Vi don't know. Won't you tell me what's been bothering you today?"

Kalil paled. To Adder's mingled joy and disappointment, he cuddled closer and buried his face in Adder's neck once more. Adder rested his cheek on Kalil's tangled hair and breathed in his lover's musky-sweet scent. "Talk to me, my darling K. Please."

Kalil's chest hitched. "I really love being in this band," he confessed in a hoarse whisper. "I'm scared that when we break up, I'll have to leave, and I don't want to."

Adder's heart turned over hard. He clutched Kalil to him as tight as he could. "That won't happen. I won't let it."

It didn't sound all that reassuring, even to Adder, but Kalil merely nodded. After a while, his breathing evened out and his body relaxed in Adder's arms.

Adder lay awake thinking for a long time. He couldn't shake the feeling that Kalil feared more than just being booted from the band. That perhaps he dreaded what he clearly saw as an inevitable breakup with Adder even more.

The idea gave Adder a strange, melting sensation in the pit of his stomach. Of all his past lovers, not one had been what Kalil was to him. Not even Vi. If Kalil felt the same way—and

Adder's every instinct said he did—then Adder's reassurance must have sounded like a pledge that they'd stay together for always.

It frightened Adder a bit to think Kalil may have gotten that idea. What absolutely terrified him, however, was the distinct feeling that he'd *meant* it that way.

Lying there in the dark, with Kalil slumbering in his embrace, Adder made a vow to himself, and to his lover—that whatever they had between them, he was not going to let it wither and die without a fight. He had no idea if he was capable of maintaining the sort of relationship he and Kalil seemed to have fallen into, but by all the gods he would throw his heart and soul into the effort.

His mind made up, Adder shut his eyes and let the soft sound of Kalil's breathing lull him to sleep.

Chapter Ten

For most people, a loud, grungy bar would be an unacceptable place for a business meeting. But Jordan, Adder and his band were not most people, and Vicious Sid's was one of their favorite bars.

Adder sipped his beer while Jordan tapped on the keys of her laptop. "You said Wilmington was the last stop in our mini-tour, correct?"

"Yes. And this is where you're booked." Jordan leaned back against the tattered red leather seat of the semicircular booth and gestured at the laptop perched on the scarred table. "Take a look."

Waving away a curl of cigarette smoke from the booth next to theirs, Adder leaned against Jordan's shoulder and peered at the screen. "The Soapbox? Oh my." He winked at her. "Jordan, my love, you're a genius."

The punk-flavored Christmas music playing over the bar's sound system nearly drowned out Kalil's growl, but not quite. Adder slipped his arm around his lover's shoulders and squeezed. The poor dear still hadn't gotten over his jealousy of Jordan, in spite of Adder's best efforts over the last month to convince him that Adder wasn't currently sleeping with anyone else, including Jordan.

Adder forced back a laugh. If someone had told him six months ago that he'd be happily monogamous, he'd have called them crazy. Life was a wild, unpredictable thing. Which was what he loved best about it.

Vi scooted onto Harpo's lap and leaned over to look at Jordan's laptop. "The Soapbox is supposed to be one of the hottest venues in Wilmington. I can't believe you got us booked there."

"What she said." Harpo put both arms around Vi and hugged her so hard she squealed. "Man, I'm really psyched about this tour. You've got us booked at all the best places."

"It was easy. Everyone wants you." Jordan's eyes cut sideways in a sly look whose meaning even the most oblivious person couldn't have missed, and Adder was far from oblivious. "So. There's your pre-TART tour in a nutshell. One month, sixteen shows in major cities across the country. The Soapbox will be the last one before the festival. The tour schedule's a little hectic, but it shouldn't wear you down too much since it's short."

"It looks great, Jordan. Thanks."

Kalil's voice betrayed only a hint of the hardness Adder knew he'd see in those dark eyes if he looked. He shook his head. For the first time in his life, he was in a relationship to which he'd been—thus far—one hundred percent faithful. And what did he get for his trouble? Jealousy and suspicion.

Not that Kalil had accused Adder of straying. Far from it. In fact, the stubborn darling continued to insist that he wasn't jealous, and in any case they hadn't promised to be exclusive to each other so what did it matter anyway?

Adder turned and pressed a soft kiss to the side of Kalil's head. It mattered to him, whatever his sweet Special K might think. Adder took pride in his own unexpected yet surprisingly welcome ability to be true to one person. And despite Kalil's words, Adder knew he was Kalil's only lover now.

The knowledge gave him a quiet joy of a kind he'd never dreamed existed a few short months ago. It might not last forever—what did, in the end?—but he and Kalil had a good thing together. That was enough, for now.

Someone stumbled against the side of the booth, splattering beer on Kalil's arm. Shooting a withering glare at the offending drunk, Kalil grabbed a napkin and blotted his T-shirt. Adder watched him with a smile. He adored Kalil's volatile temper. Perverse, maybe, but true.

Kalil tilted his face up and gave Adder a heart-stopping smile when he noticed his gaze. "What're you thinking about?"

"You, darling. Specifically, sitting on your cock and riding you until we both die of exhaustion." It wasn't entirely a lie, since Adder tended to daydream about precisely that at inappropriate times. He laughed at the way lust flared in Kalil's eyes even as he blushed like a schoolgirl. "My goodness, look at the time. We should really be getting home."

Kalil's eyebrows went up. He glanced at the clock over the bar, which read nine p.m., and grinned. "Yeah. I'm really anxious to, um...get to bed."

Heat pooled between Adder's legs. Gods, but it *did* things to him when Kalil's voice went low and husky like that. What he wouldn't give to push Kalil's knees apart, kneel on the beer-splashed floor between his legs and suck him off right here in the middle of the Friday-night party crowd.

Jordan's hand landed on his shoulder. "Adder, I'd like to discuss something with you, if you don't mind."

Planting a swift kiss on Kalil's lips, Adder turned to Jordan. "Of course. What is it?"

She glanced around. "It's private, actually."

Adder considered. He thought he knew what she might say to him, and his instinct was to say no. However, she held their professional lives in her hand. He didn't truly believe she'd hold that over him for mere sex, but he wasn't inclined to take chances where his band's career was concerned. Which meant that despite his longing to dive into bed with Kalil and never emerge again, he was going to stay and at least hear Jordan out.

"All right." Adder took Kalil's hand in his and kissed his knuckles. "Keep the bed warm for me, darling?"

Kalil narrowed his eyes, as if he knew what this private talk was about and didn't like it one bit. "Adder, what—"

Adder darted forward and kissed Kalil before he could say anything else. "I'll be home soon. Promise."

"Fine." Sliding to the edge of the booth, Kalil pushed to his feet. "Come on, guys."

Vi and Harpo exchanged indecipherable looks. "Um. Okay." Vi climbed off Harpo's lap and slid out of the booth. "Bye, Jordan. Adder, see you at home."

Adder watched Kalil's face as he threaded his way through the crowd. Those dark eyes snapped with the anger he never expressed out loud, and the soft lips which parted so sweetly for Adder's tongue every night were pressed into a thin line.

Adder stifled a sigh. He didn't mind having a possessive lover, but a possessive lover who denied his own possessiveness was exhausting.

When Kalil, Vi and Harpo were out of sight, Adder turned to Jordan with a smile. "So. What was this private matter you needed to discuss with me?"

She rested her chin in one hand and gave him a keen look. "What's going on with you and Kalil?"

It wasn't exactly what Adder had expected to hear. He blinked. "We're fucking. I thought you knew that."

"Well, no one's actually told me that. But I knew anyway." She arched an eyebrow at him. "It's pretty obvious."

Adder shook his head. "Then I'm afraid I don't know what you mean."

"What I mean is, how serious is it? Are you *just* fucking, or is it something more?"

Now *that* was the hundred-million-dollar question, wasn't it? Adder knew the answer, for himself at any rate. But he wasn't sure if he should tell Jordan. Adder refused to believe she would drop them—she was far too much of a professional for that—but if she knew Adder considered himself off limits her support for them might cool, even if she didn't intend it to.

For the first time in his memory, Adder wished he had a bit less sexual magnetism. If Jordan wasn't attracted to him, he wouldn't have to walk this particular tightrope.

Letting his eyelids fall to half-mast, he gave her a smile which could be construed as seductive if one were inclined to see it that way. "How could Kalil and I be serious about one another? This is the rock-and-roll lifestyle, darling, there's no such thing as exclusive."

To his surprise, she burst out laughing. "Adder, honey, you're a doll, but I'm not in the market for a kid half my age to take to bed."

Relieved—and, if he were honest with himself, somewhat miffed—Adder leaned against the back of the booth. "In that case, I must confess that at this point in time, I don't wish to be with anyone besides Kalil."

She nodded, as if she'd already guessed as much. "And what about him? How does he feel?"

“I don’t know. But I do know he doesn’t have sex with anyone but me, and I honestly don’t believe he wants to.” He smiled, remembering the way Kalil’s cheeks heated and his jaw clenched whenever he caught a would-be groupie coming on to Adder. “He’s very jealous. It’s rather flattering, really.”

Jordan snorted. “Yes, I’d noticed that about him. I think he still sees me as a rival for your affections.”

Raucous laughter erupted from a nearby table. Adder leaned closer to Jordan to make himself heard over the noise. “Jordan, this may seem like a strange question, but why are you asking about my relationship with Kalil if you’ve no intention of bedding me?”

Her gaze turned thoughtful. “Intra-band romance can be a very good thing, or a very bad thing, depending. I have no personal problem with you and Kalil getting together. But as your manager, I have a responsibility to look out for you. I just want to know if this is something I should be concerned about.”

Adder glanced around the bar, trying to think of the best way to phrase it. Jordan closed her laptop and waited, hands folded on the table.

“I don’t think you need to be concerned,” Adder answered after a moment. “Kalil and I are together and exclusive for now, and we’re enjoying one another. But we’ve already discussed the future, and we both believe we can remain on friendly and professional terms if we tire of our current situation.” He smiled. The truth had been stretched, but not broken. Kalil would be proud, if he ever found out about it. Which Adder was not at all sure was a good idea.

“Good.” Jordan patted Adder’s cheek. “Okay, I’m heading home. Do you need a ride?”

“No, that’s all right, I’ll call a taxi. I can’t ask you to drive all the way across town.”

"A taxi'll cost a fortune in this traffic, and I'm going in your direction anyway." Scooting out of the booth, she tucked her laptop under one arm and held out the other hand to Adder. "Come on, hon. I'll drive you."

He grinned. "Yes, Mommy."

She rolled her eyes as Adder exited the booth and took her hand. "Brat."

"But I'm a *lovable* brat." He fluttered his eyelashes at her.

The both laughed as she led him through the growing press of night owls and out into the frigid December air. Adder slid into the passenger seat of Jordan's Mercedes feeling much lighter of heart than he had when she first asked him to stay and talk.

I'll tell Kalil that she's not interested in sleeping with me. That should make him happy.

Thus decided, Adder settled in and watched the traffic go by. He couldn't wait to get home and see the look on Kalil's face.

Unfortunately, the very first expression which greeted Adder on his arrival home over an hour later was one of incandescent fury.

"Where the *fuck* have you been?" Kalil demanded the moment Adder walked in. "It's been almost an hour and a half!"

Adder took a swift look around. A Larrikin Love tune floated down the hall from Vi's room. Harpo's favorite jacket was missing from the hook on the wall, which meant he must be at Sheila's. *So K and I are free to fight. Oh, joy.*

With a cautious smile, Adder deposited his keys on the table beside the door. "I'm sorry, darling. There was a three-vehicle wreck on Peachtree, and it had traffic backed up on all the side roads as well. We'd still be stuck in the traffic jam if

Jordan didn't know this city as well as she does. She used alleys and parking lots, for goodness' sake. It was impressive."

"Uh-huh. Sure." Kalil crossed his arms and glared. "Did you fuck her?"

Torn between shock and outrage, Adder gaped. "My dear Special K, did I not tell you before that I had no intention of having sexual relations with Jordan?"

"Yeah, I know what you said. But I see how you and her look at each other." Kalil uncrossed his arms and started pacing. "Just tell me the fucking truth."

"I *am* telling you the truth, K." Frustrated, Adder raked the hair out of his eyes. "I did not fuck Jordan. I *will* not fuck Jordan, even if she wanted me to, which *by the way* she does not. We did get that little misconception cleared up tonight, at least."

Kalil met Adder's glower with one of his own. "So, what, she said 'oh hey Adder, just wanted to let you know I don't want to fuck you'? Uh-huh. I just bet."

A sudden surge of anger heated Adder's blood. Stalking forward, he grabbed Kalil's shoulders and shook him. "How *dare* you accuse me of... Whatever the bloody *fuck* is it you're accusing me of?" Kalil opened his mouth. Adder plowed on, cutting off whatever pitiful protests Kalil was about to spew forth. "All this time, ever since Halloween, you've been swearing up and down that it doesn't matter whether or not we're exclusive, yet you have the fucking *nerve* to yell at me because you *think* I slept with Jordan, after I just *told* you I didn't?"

A bitter smile curved Kalil's lips. "Yeah, because you're known for always telling the unvarnished truth, aren't you?"

That hit home, mostly because it wasn't an unfounded accusation. Adder shoved Kalil away, hard. "My dear, you are cordially invited to go fuck yourself."

Adder turned and stomped down the hall to the bedroom, fuming. Gods, why did Kalil have to be so damned difficult?

He tried to slam the bedroom door behind him. Kalil's arm got in the way.

Gritting his teeth, Adder whirled around and tried to shove Kalil back into the hall. "Go away, you unmitigated ass."

In answer, Kalil muscled his way inside and stood well within Adder's personal space, shaking all over. "Look, I…I'm sorry, okay? I just…I guess I…"

He trailed off, worried gaze searching Adder's face. Lingering indignation helped Adder resist the urge to cuddle him. "Yes?"

Kalil hung his head and chewed one thumbnail. "It just bugs me to think of you being with anyone else. And she wants you. I can tell."

There it was, at last. Adder looped his arms around Kalil's neck. "I know it bothers you, darling. But you truly have nothing to worry about with Jordan. She told me straight out this evening that she didn't want me like that."

A frown creased Kalil's forehead, clashing rather strongly with the relief in his eyes. "But she's always flirting with you."

"True." Adder shrugged. "I believe that's simply her way of interacting with those she feels would be receptive."

The corners of Kalil's mouth turned up. "Sounds like someone else I know."

"Indeed." Cupping Kalil's cheek in one hand, Adder peered hard into his eyes. "Listen to me, K. Nothing lasts forever. But right now, you are the only one I want."

An indecipherable expression fleeted across Kalil's face and was gone before Adder could grasp it. Kalil smiled. "Mutual, you freak."

Smiling back at Kalil, Adder buried a hand in Kalil's hair, bent and kissed him. Kalil's mouth opened on a soft moan, his arms coming up to slide around Adder's neck. Adder crushed him close and soaked up the feel of Kalil's warm, solid body pressed tight against his.

By the time the kiss broke, Adder's cock felt like a shaft of solid stone in his snug green corduroys. He rested his forehead against Kalil's, one hand still tangled in his hair and the other clamped onto his ass. His entire body ached and his voice didn't appear to work. Strange, how his desire for Kalil was invariably so strong it shut down his higher mental processes. That had never happened with any of his past lovers.

Kalil's sweet mouth curved into a sinful smile. "Didn't you say something earlier about riding my cock?"

What little blood remained in Adder's brain at that point promptly drained southward. Locking his arms around Kalil's waist, Adder hauled him to the bed, threw him across the mattress and plopped down on top of him. He settled himself between Kalil's legs and attacked the stretch of bared neck with his teeth.

Kalil let out a yelp. "Whoa, damn! Hang on a minute." Fingers dug into Adder's hair and pulled his head up. Kalil grinned at him. "I think getting naked might be helpful if we're gonna fuck."

Despite the almost unbearable need to mark Kalil's throat with a necklace of purple bruises, Adder had to concede his point. In order to get Kalil's magnificent prick inside him, both of their pants would have to come down. And as long as they had to undress that far, they may as well take off everything. Fucking with clothes on had a certain illicit appeal, but that tended to fade with familiarity. Besides, Adder loved the feel of Kalil's bare skin against his own.

With one last quick nip to Kalil's collarbone, Adder pushed up to a kneeling position. He kicked off his shoes, tore his glittery red sweater over his head and went to work on the pants. He got them halfway down his thighs, then crashed onto his side and managed to drag them the rest of the way off.

Laughing, Kalil undid his jeans and tugged them off. "Graceful."

Adder pounced on him, pinning his wrists above his head. "When did you take off your shirt? I wanted to help."

"No, you wanted to tie my hands together with it like you did last week." Kalil wriggled delightfully under Adder's weight. "Let me go, you crazy bastard, I have to get the lube."

"Stay. I'll get it."

Before Kalil could protest, Adder rolled off him and reached for the bedside table. Ignoring the tube of cinnamon-flavored gel sitting beside the lamp, he dug the little bottle of liquid lube—"favored by the biggest names in gay porn", if the label was to be believed—out of the drawer. He set the bottle beside Kalil's hand, straddled his face and dove for his crotch.

Kalil let out a squeak when Adder's mouth closed around his cock. "Oh. God."

Adder hummed his agreement around a mouthful of delicious dick. Kalil's tongue caught the tip of Adder's cock. He raised his hips away from Kalil's searching mouth and grasping hand. As many times as they'd done this, Kalil no doubt knew what Adder wanted, and it wasn't a mutual suck.

After a few seconds, Kalil evidently caught on. The mattress squeaked as he flopped backward. Adder rewarded him by relaxing his gag reflex and pushed downward until his nose dug into Kalil's balls.

He stayed there, throat working, a firm hand on Kalil's hipbone to keep him still. When his lungs began to burn from lack of air, Adder drew slowly back and breathed in his lover's ripe, musky scent. He spent a long, glorious time lapping up the little droplets of precome as they oozed one by one from the slit in the head of Kalil's cock. The way Kalil whimpered and squirmed with every swipe of Adder's tongue was an addiction Adder had acquired early on and had no intention of doing without now.

When the whimpers became inarticulate pleas for more-more-more, Adder let Kalil's cock part his lips and fill his mouth. Through the onslaught of taste and smell and sensation, Adder heard the click of the lube bottle being opened. He let out a muffled moan. His anus clenched and fluttered. The anticipation of that first touch undid him nearly as much as the touch itself.

But not quite, he thought when Kalil pushed two slick fingers inside him. Those clever fingertips unerringly searched out his prostate and gave it a firm rub, and all thought vanished like fog in the sunshine. Adder rocked backward and forward, again and again. The thrill of being penetrated from both ends made his blood sing.

All too soon, the probing fingers withdrew from Adder's hole and a warm hand slapped his ass. "S-stop," Kalil breathed. "Too close."

A large part of Adder did not want to take his mouth from Kalil's cock. A much larger part, however, wanted the aforementioned cock up his ass immediately, if not sooner. Kalil was an inventive lover, and quite astonishingly flexible, but even he couldn't manage to have his cock in two places at once.

Adder pushed himself upward. Kalil's prick hit his belly with a wet smack, splattering Adder's face with saliva and pre-come. Wiping a bit of fluid from the corner of his eye, Adder rose to his knees and turned to face the other direction. He smiled at the sight of Kalil lying there flushed and panting, brown eyes hazed with desire.

Leaning forward, Adder planted his hands on either side of Kalil's head and brushed their mouths together in the barest whisper of a kiss. Kalil arched up to meet him, head tilting sideways and hands delving into Adder's hair. His arms shook, and his breath came fast and harsh through his nose.

Adder happily surrendered to Kalil's obvious hunger. It was a heady feeling, being wanted this much by someone who knew him not as a star, but as a person, and chose to be with him anyway. So much better than a full-time groupie's skillful but passionless touch, or the desperate adoration of fans who sought to gain their idol's notice through sex.

Shifting his weight to one hand, Adder groped along the line of Kalil's body to grasp his rigid shaft. Kalil moaned into Adder's mouth, his hips canting upward in an attempt to fuck Adder's hand. Adder did his best to maneuver himself into position without breaking the kiss, but he couldn't quite manage. Frustrated and impatient, he tore his mouth from Kalil's, lined up Kalil's cock with his hole, and impaled himself in one swift motion.

Kalil's body bowed off the mattress. "Ah, oh fuck! Oh. Fuck. Nngh."

Adder agreed with that sentiment, but the pleasure-pain of the quick, barely lubed penetration stole his breath and rendered him speechless. He dug his fingers into Kalil's chest and rocked in place while his body adjusted to the sudden fullness.

Kalil's hands smoothed over Adder's thighs. "Okay?" His voice came out rough and thick, but concern shone through the lust in his eyes.

Adder managed a shaky smile. "Good. It's good." He

seesawed his hips. Kalil's cock shifted inside him, tearing identical gasps from them both. "Gods. Move."

Grunting with the effort, Kalil thrust upward hard enough to make Adder bounce.

It wasn't enough. Judging by Kalil's frustrated whine, he realized it too. He clamped both hands onto Adder's hipbones. "Hang on."

Adder snaked his arms around Kalil's neck just in time to keep himself from flopping over like a rag doll when Kalil rolled them sideways. The room spun for a moment. When it settled, Adder lay on his back, with his legs around Kalil's waist and Kalil's prick still firmly embedded in his ass.

Laughing, Adder pulled Kalil's face down for a kiss. "Caveman."

Kalil grinned. "I'll show you caveman."

Adder's snicker melted into a groan when Kalil hooked his powerful drummer's arms under Adder's knees and started pounding into him. Adder clung to Kalil's muscular shoulders with all his strength. "Gods, yes. Harder. Fuck me harder."

He got a growl and a vicious thrust in response. Pain nipped Adder's insides with tiny kitten teeth, just enough to turn his rising excitement sharp and urgent. Reaching one hand behind him, Adder grasped the headboard. He curled his other hand around his cock and started jerking himself off. It wouldn't take much at this point, just a few strokes and he'd come.

From the half-pained look on Kalil's face, he was just as close. Seized by a sudden need to watch Kalil come *right now*, Adder twisted his upper body at an anatomically incorrect angle, reared up and clamped his teeth onto Kalil's left nipple.

"Fucking *shit*!" Kalil drove his prick into Adder twice more, hard and quick, then went still. A violent shudder ran through his body.

The pulse and swell of his cock sent Adder tumbling over the precipice alongside his lover. He let go of Kalil's nipple and cried out when his orgasm blasted through him, painting his chest and stomach with sticky warmth.

Kalil pulled out of Adder's ass, dropped his legs and collapsed in a heap, his face buried in the curve of Adder's neck. Adder locked both arms around Kalil and held him close. His heart galloped against Adder's sternum, and his breath puffed warm and soft on the skin of Adder's throat.

Smiling, Adder nuzzled Kalil's mussed and sweaty hair. Moments like this one—lying tangled in bed with Kalil naked in his arms, basking in the golden afterglow of glorious sex—made all the petty arguments and inconveniences of a relationship seem unimportant.

"Goddamn," Kalil mumbled after several minutes of silent, sated recovery. "Why is it that sex after a fight is always so fucking intense?"

"Adrenaline, darling. We feel everything much more keenly on an adrenaline rush." Adder had no idea if he was right, but it sounded plausible, and that was good enough for him.

Kalil laughed. "It was a rhetorical question, dumbass. You can stop guessing."

"What makes you think I'm guessing?" Adder trailed his fingertips down Kalil's spine and back up again. "Perhaps I'm an expert on human physiology."

Lifting his head, Kalil gave Adder a heart-thumping smile. "You know what, that wouldn't surprise me at this point."

For some reason, Adder's throat closed up. Bereft of speech, he chose to express his feelings by cradling Kalil's lovely, sex-flushed face in his hands and pressing a reverent kiss to those soft, sweet lips. They opened with a near-silent sigh. Adder shut his eyes and reveled in the slick slide of Kalil's tongue against his.

When they pulled apart at last, Adder let his eyelids flutter open, only to be pinned by Kalil's solemn stare. Something in Kalil's expression made Adder's stomach clench. He frowned. "What is it, love?"

Kalil opened his mouth, shut it again, then shook his head. "You're really not sleeping with Jordan?"

Adder met Kalil's gaze and held it, doing his best to drop all the shields he usually kept between himself and the world to let Kalil see straight down to his soul. "I'm not, Kalil. I swear it."

Kalil nodded, and relief washed over Adder like a tidal wave. He had no idea why Kalil's belief and trust was so important to him, but there it was.

Shifting his weight, Kalil rested his forehead against Adder's. His hand lifted to caress Adder's cheek. "She still wants you, you know."

Adder twisted a lock of Kalil's hair around one finger. "She told me she doesn't. I believe her."

Silence. Kalil stroked Adder's jaw, his hairline, the shell of his ear. Adder could hear him breathing in the quiet. Vi's music bled through the closed door, a faint soundtrack to a largely unspoken drama.

"People say a lot of things," Kalil whispered after a long, long time. "They don't always mean them."

Adder had no answer for that, since he knew it to be true. Unwilling to offer reassurance based on lies—and what a sea change *that* was for a spinner of fictions such as himself—Adder gathered his lover close and kissed him with more passion than before.

Eventually, their mutual need rose high enough to drown all the things they hadn't said.

Chapter Eleven

"Christ on a bike, would you look at this place?"

"You said it, Harpo." Walking through the gate which separated the parking area from the TART Festival grounds, Kalil stared around in something close to awe. They'd come in through the entrance reserved for talent and festival workers, so this was their first sight of the grounds, and it was pretty impressive. He nodded toward a huge royal blue tent about ten yards from where they stood, the last in a double row of them. "Is that a disco?"

"The sign over the entrance does indeed read 'disco'." Adder's arms slid around Kalil from behind, and warm lips sucked gently on his earlobe. "Come dancing with me tonight."

"Okay." Grinning, Kalil tilted his head up and sideways to kiss the angle of Adder's jaw. "But if you make them play 'Vogue' and do that stupid-ass dance, I'm pretending I don't know you."

Adder pressed a tragic hand to his brow. "You cut me to the quick, darling."

Reaching backward, Kalil wound an arm around Adder's neck. "Yeah, poor you."

Adder smiled. "Kiss it better?"

Kalil happily obliged. Adder hummed into Kalil's mouth,

one hand caressing his belly through his T-shirt.

Before things could get too heated, Vi grabbed them both and hugged them hard, then bounced off toward the tents in a flurry of purple gauze. "Oh my God, y'all, check it out. They have a comedy club and a yoga studio. Oh *shit*, and a massage tent!" Vi squealed and clapped her hands. "Jordan, this is fucking awesome."

Jordan laughed as she joined the group. "Thank you. My partners and I are pretty proud of how it turned out."

"I don't blame you." Adder drew away from Kalil, pulled Jordan into his arms and kissed her forehead. "This festival is going to be magnificent, love. I'm sure I speak for all of us when I say we are happy and proud to be playing here."

Kalil murmured his agreement along with Harpo and Vi, but his heart was only half in it. For nearly nine months, he'd been looking forward to playing the TART Festival. And now here they were, at the festival grounds, just over forty-eight hours shy of the biggest show of their career so far. Why did Adder have to throw a wet blanket on Kalil's excitement by flaunting his closeness to Jordan?

Kalil scowled, disgusted with himself. After all this time, he still hadn't managed to shake off the urge to snarl every time Adder hugged Jordan, or she kissed his cheek. Hell, every time the two of them got involved in a marathon game of Monopoly, Kalil burned with jealousy. It was embarrassing. Especially since as far as he could tell, Adder hadn't slept with anyone but him for the better part of a year.

God. Had it really been that long? Kalil shook his head. It amazed him that they'd stayed together this long. He wanted to believe that Adder restricting himself to one lover for ten whole months was the amazing part. But the truth was, Kalil had surprised himself as well. Adder was the first person he'd ever *wanted* to stay with for an extended length of time.

Kind of scary, that.

Jordan's laughter jolted him out of his reverie. He glanced over just in time to see Jordan slip her arm around Adder's waist and give him a squeeze. Adder rested an arm on Jordan's shoulders. He didn't look at Kalil.

Fuming, Kalil followed Vi down the wide avenue between two rows of colorful tents. He was glad his sunglasses hid his eyes, because he'd be fucked if he'd let Adder see that the thing with Jordan still bugged him.

Footsteps pounded behind him. "Dude, wait up."

Kalil stopped and waited for Harpo to catch up. Once he drew even with Kalil, the two of them started walking again. Up ahead, Vi stopped to talk to a woman in a long gold dress. Kalil ignored them as he and Harpo passed by. Harpo grinned and waved.

After a rainy morning, the afternoon had turned fine and hot. Steam rose from the ground as the wet grass dried in the sunshine. The air smelled of damp earth and oncoming summer. Kalil felt some of his Jordan-related tension draining away as he and Harpo strolled along in companionable silence.

They walked past at least a dozen tents, all crawling with vendors setting up for the festival. Music drifted from all directions, and people called greetings to them as they walked. Eventually, they left the vendor booths behind and emerged into a wide meadow with a stage on the other side.

Kalil stopped in the middle of the field and gazed at the stage. "This is where we're playing, right?"

"The Gandhi stage. Yep. The main stage is over there someplace, I think." Harpo waved a vague hand to his right. "So. What's up?"

Kalil shrugged. “Nothing.”

“Uh-huh. ’Cause you always brood like this.” Harpo rubbed the stubble on his jaw. “Come to think of it, you *do* always brood like this lately.”

“I do not,” Kalil protested, even though he knew Harpo was right.

Harpo gave him a look that said “oh, *please*” loud and clear. “Kalil, I’ve known you for ten years. This right here…” he patted Kalil’s cheek, “…is the patented Special K Pout.”

Kalil swatted Harpo’s hand away. “Shut up.”

Harpo just laughed. The bastard. “Come on, man, what’s your problem? You don’t still think Adder and Jordan are playing hide the pickle, do you?”

“Did you just say ‘hide the pickle’?”

“Did you just avoid the question?”

Sighing, Kalil sat on the cool grass and wrapped his arms around his knees. “No. I mean, no, I know Adder’s not sleeping with Jordan. I know they’re just really good friends, but…” He trailed off, toying with the bike chain bracelet Adder had bought him in San Francisco and trying to find a way to articulate what he felt.

“But, knowing something and *knowing* something are two different things.” Harpo sat cross-legged on the ground beside Kalil and grinned at the incredulous look Kalil gave him. “Been working on my mind-reading powers.” He held both hands out in front of him and waggled his fingers.

Kalil laughed. “Yeah, well, I guess you’re right. It bothers me that they’re so close. Which is *stupid*, I know.”

“It is, kind of.” A large green grasshopper landed on the leg of Harpo’s jeans. He brushed it off. “But hey, you’re a jealous person when it comes to relationships. Always have been.”

Kalil wanted to argue, but Harpo was right. Every guy Kalil had ever been with for more than a couple of weeks said the same damn thing.

Frustrated with Adder, with himself and with relationships in general, Kalil rested his forehead on his knees. “Goddammit.”

Harpo squeezed Kalil’s shoulder. Kalil was ridiculously grateful for his friend’s silent support. It helped to know that *someone* understood how he felt, because he sure as hell didn’t.

“You’re too possessive,” Vi shouted at Kalil over the thump of seventies dance music at the disco toward dawn the next morning. “And he’s not possessive enough. Makes for hard feelings, if you ask me.”

“Nobody asked you.” Tightening his grip on Vi’s hips, Kalil ground his crotch against her backside. He glanced at Adder, who had coaxed Harpo onto the dance floor and was busy twirling him around in a weird hybrid of a dry hump and a waltz. “Jesus, if Sheila was here she’d tear both their balls off with her teeth.”

“Yeah. But she’s not, thank God.” Vi spun in Kalil’s embrace and wound her arms around his neck. “Stop changing the subject.”

“There’s a subject?”

She shook her head. “Men. You’re all completely clueless.”

“Naw. We just make you think that so you’ll do our laundry.”

Vi laughed. “Kalil. Stop avoiding this discussion.”

The Donna Summer tune booming through the speakers morphed into something slow and sensual that Kalil didn’t recognize. Sighing, he pulled Vi close and pressed his cheek to her hair. "Okay, what discussion are we having?"

"We are discussing your relationship with Adder, you jackass."

"Oh yeah. That." He'd rather whack his balls with a hammer a few times than have yet another talk about his and Adder's relationship, but he wasn't about to tell Vi that. She wouldn't listen unless he was ugly about it, and he couldn't bring himself to be mean to someone he loved like a sister. "What about it?"

"It's unbalanced, that's what."

"Unbalanced?"

"Yeah. Like I said before, you're too possessive, and he's not possessive enough. Unbalanced."

Kalil peered through the heaving press of bodies to where Adder was now slow dancing with a girl who looked like she didn't even remember what planet she was on. The sight made Kalil's gut burn. "I see your point."

"Uh-huh." Vi drew back enough to look Kalil in the eye. Her expression was solemn. "If you and Adder are going to last, something has to change. Y'all have to restore the balance."

"How are we supposed to restore something we never had?" Kalil's stomach flip-flopped when he realized what else Vi had said. "And what the hell makes you think either one of us is looking for anything long term?"

She snorted. "You've been together almost a year. For Adder, that's not just long term, it's a fucking lifetime. Trust me, he wants this thing with you to last. He just doesn't know how to make that happen."

Kalil stumbled to a stop and stared at Vi in shock. He couldn't decide whether to drag her outside where it was relatively quiet and grill her or pretend he hadn't heard. She cocked an eyebrow at him as if she knew exactly what he was thinking.

Before he could make up his mind what—if anything—to say about this new development, a pair of hands grabbed him and ripped him away from Vi. Irritated, he turned and aimed a scowl at his assailant. "Harpo, what the fuck?"

"Dude, you have to let me dance with Vi." Harpo darted a panicky gaze around the room. "All the guys are hitting on me ever since they saw that asshole Adder *groping* me."

"What, you can't fight 'em off?"

Harpo glared. Kalil snickered.

Vi let out a long-suffering sigh, grabbed Harpo's wrist and yanked him toward her. "Fine, Harpo. Come on. And you." She pointed a finger at Kalil. "Go get Adder away from that drunk girl before he gets in trouble. And remember what I said, yeah?"

Thus dismissed, Kalil obediently wove his way through the writhing tangle of bodies to where Adder swayed to the music with that shitfaced little slut draped around his neck like a scarf. Kalil thought about tapping the girl on the shoulder and politely asking if he could cut in, but decided against it. Even if Kalil could manage politeness right now—which he wasn't sure he could—the kid probably wouldn't notice. She seemed barely able to stand, never mind respond to what anyone said.

Tamping down his irrational anger, Kalil touched Adder's arm. "Hey, Adder."

Turning, Adder gave Kalil a thousand-watt smile. "Hello, darling. Did you need something?"

Kalil shrugged. "Harpo stole Vi. Dance with me?"

The way Adder's face lit up told Kalil things that scared him to death and made his spirit fly at the same time. "Of course.

One moment.” Lifting the drunk girl’s chin, Adder grinned at her. “I’m sorry, dear, but my lover desires my company on the dance floor. I must oblige him.”

The girl’s rounded features twisted into what was probably supposed to be a sneer. “Whatever. F’ckoff.” She pushed away from Adder and staggered off through the throng.

Adder shook his head, amusement in his eyes. “I will never understand why people wish to incapacitate themselves. How can anyone enjoy themselves when they have no control over their actions and won’t be able to remember it later?”

“Don’t know, don’t care.” Kalil reached up and clasped his arms around Adder’s neck. “I just want to dance.”

Smiling, Adder pulled Kalil close and kissed his forehead. “Of course, my darling.”

As he looked into Adder’s eyes, Kalil’s heart lurched. Vi was right, he realized. Adder wanted to stay with him for the long haul. Which was surprising, but not nearly as surprising as the realization that he wanted the same thing.

It was enough to give a guy a massive headache. Kalil rested his head in the curve of Adder’s neck, shut his eyes and tried not to think about it. There’d be plenty of time for relationship work later.

If the two of them didn’t manage to fuck it up in the meantime.

He tried not to think about *that* either.

Kalil relaxed his throat and swallowed Adder’s prick as deep as he could. Adder groaned, fingers clenching a double handful of Kalil’s hair. “Oh gods. Yes. Almost there.”

Encouraged, Kalil sucked harder. Adder rewarded him with a ragged gasp and a flood of semen in his mouth. He swallowed until the spurting stopped, then let go of Adder's cock and clambered to his feet just as Adder dropped to his knees.

Kalil had his cock out and down Adder's throat in no time. Propping himself against the wall of the trailer the festival had provided for the band, Kalil closed his eyes and concentrated on getting off as fast as possible. They were supposed to be backstage in less than twenty minutes, and they had a ways to walk to get there.

Thankfully, it didn't take long for Kalil to come. He muffled his cries behind the hand not clutching Adder's hair in a death grip. Adder gulped Kalil's semen, then sat back on his heels with a smug grin.

"I am going to kill you," Kalil declared once he got his breath back.

"For what? Sucking your cock?" Adder rose to his feet, wiping his mouth on the back of his hand. "Darling, please. I know better."

Kalil shot Adder a glare as they both tucked their pricks into their pants and zipped up. "I can't believe you dragged me in here for sex when you know damn well we need to be way the hell on the other side of the festival grounds in..." Kalil glanced at his watch and nearly had a heart attack. "Fucking shit. We have to be there in ten minutes."

Adder waved one hand in a gesture of supreme unconcern. "We are the talent, my dear. We're allowed use of the backstage transport, remember?"

The truth was, Kalil had forgotten all about the complimentary golf carts in which TART workers drove artists and press from place to place. But he wasn't telling Adder that.

"Yeah, okay, fine." Kalil scanned the trailer floor. "You

swallowed it all, right?" Vi had threatened them both with death and/or castration if they got spunk on the floor and she stepped in it. Knowing her like he did, he didn't much want to find out the hard way whether or not she was serious.

"Of course." Adder gave him a withering look. "Notice I did not ask *you* such a ridiculous question."

Kalil decided not to answer that. Grabbing his sunglasses from the table, he slipped them on. "Let's roll. Jordan'll kill us if we're late."

They linked hands and walked out into the late-afternoon sunshine. Adder flagged down a golf cart only a few yards down the dusty dirt lane which skirted the perimeter of the festival grounds. He and Kalil climbed in, and the cart bumped off down the road.

To Kalil, it felt like the ride took forever. He knew it was just his nerves talking, but he couldn't help breathing a sigh of relief when they reached the back of the Gandhi stage and he realized the previous band was still playing.

"Where the fuck have you been?" Harpo demanded when Adder and Kalil climbed the stairs into the wings. "We're gonna have to start setting up in, like, two minutes!"

Adder took Harpo's hand in his free one and squeezed it. "Relax, love. We're here now."

Kalil was pretty sure whatever Harpo said next was less than complimentary, but he couldn't tell for certain since the band onstage finished their last song at that moment and the crowd went wild. Vi, who was standing as close to the stage as she could get without actually being on it, squealed and applauded along with the audience.

"Thank you very much!" cried the singer, a wisp of a boy with a shaved, tattooed head and a pink plaid miniskirt. "We are Me & My Gay Friends, and this show is dedicated to TPig!

Fight the thought police, my brother!"

Kalil grinned. The bands he'd seen in the last day and a half had been interesting, to say the least. He kind of wished he hadn't missed this one.

The band exited the stage on the opposite side. Roadies scurried in their wake, breaking down their equipment. Vi turned from the stage and wandered over to join Kalil, Adder and Harpo. "God, I love that band. Spencer is *so* cute."

"Which one's Spencer?" Kalil asked, letting go of Adder's hand.

"The singer." Vi leaned against Harpo with a deep sigh. "Too bad he doesn't want any of what I've got."

Laughing, Adder leaned over and kissed the top of Vi's head. "Then he's missing out, my love."

"Sweet talker." She gave him a light punch in the arm, but she looked pleased. "We better start getting our shit together. Their set won't take long to break, and we go on in half an hour."

"Vi's right." Jordan strode up to them and clapped Adder on the back. "I wish you kids would let me hire roadies for you. There's no need to do all the set-up and breakdown yourself."

"Thank you, love, but we're very particular when it comes to our instruments." Adder shot a fond look in Kalil's direction. "Some more than others, of course."

Kalil just shrugged. Maybe he was being a diva—Vi had called him that more than once—but he wasn't about to apologize for insisting on setting up his own drum kit. He'd learned the hard way that no one else could do it the way he wanted.

Jordan smiled at Kalil. "Well, since the end result seems to be the best drumming I've ever heard in my life, I won't complain."

As usual, Kalil's undeniable jealousy of Jordan collided with gratification at the compliment, leaving him confused and flustered. He hunched his shoulders. "Um. Thanks."

Adder grinned, his eyes gleaming with amusement. "All right then, my dears. Let's get busy, shall we?"

Kalil went to work with the rest of them, grateful for the distraction. He hated it when Jordan looked at him with such pride, because it made him like her, and he didn't want to like her as long as she kept stealing Adder's attention from him.

Christ, you sound like a spoiled eighth-grade girl. Jordan's been nothing but nice to you, and she's done amazing things for our career as a band. Stop being an asshole.

Easier said than done, as it turned out. Kalil started to approach Jordan several times during the set-up and chickened out at the last minute. He cursed himself over and over, but all his self-reproach didn't do a damn thing to make him man up and apologize to Jordan for being a dick.

Ironically, it was Jordan herself who gave him a chance he couldn't pass up. She approached him as the band stood in the wings, listening to a young woman in a rainbow-striped polo shirt introduce them.

She walked up and stood beside Kalil, hands in her shorts pockets. "Okay there, K?"

"Yeah." He shot her a sidelong glance. She was watching the stage, a faint smile on her lips. "Um. Jordan?"

"Yes?"

"I want... That is, I think I should... I've been..."

She turned to him with a question in her eyes. He blew out a frustrated breath. "Okay, look, I know I've been kind of an ass to you, and I'm sorry."

"It's all right." She smiled. "He's really crazy about you, you know."

Kalil blinked at her. He had no idea why it surprised him that she'd told him that, but it did.

Before he could say anything, the audience exploded into cheers and applause, and he realized it was time to go on. With one final glance at Jordan, he followed his bandmates onto the stage.

Adder swayed up to the mic, sunlight and spotlights catching the silver glitter on his face and bare chest and highlighting the curves of lean muscle beneath his snug Lycra shorts. "Good afternoon, my beauties," he purred. "My name is Adder, and we"—he indicated Vi, Harpo and Kalil with a sweep of his arm—"are here for your pleasure." He beamed over his shoulder at Kalil. "If you would, my love?"

This is it. Drawing a deep, cleansing breath, Kalil tapped out the opening beats of "Starseed", and the biggest show of his career officially began.

The performance went even better than they'd expected, which was saying something considering their collective optimism about it.

Kalil practically floated to the front of the stage when Adder introduced him. The sea of people stretching the width and length of the field screamed and cried their names. Arms reached for them across the space between the barrier and the stage.

Kalil had never experienced anything like it. And he definitely wanted to experience it again. Preferably every single day for the rest of his life.

Taking Adder's hand in his left and Vi's in his right, Kalil lifted his arms into the air and bowed along with his bandmates. Vi laughed, her hand warm and damp in his. Grinning ear to ear, Kalil turned and gave her a quick peck on the lips. She beamed at him.

Buoyed by the joy in the air, Kalil freed both his hands and wrapped his arms around Adder's waist. Normally he wasn't so demonstrative on stage. But after a performance like this one, a fucking *legendary* performance, he felt bursting with affection for the whole world, and the man at his side in particular. After all, they were a team. Partners, in music and in life.

In all the months they'd lived and worked together, it was the first time Kalil had really thought of their relationship that way. The revelation left him reeling.

Tilting his head up, Kalil stared into Adder's face. Adder wasn't conventionally handsome. His face was a little too long, his body too thin, and, well, the street-urchin-meets-disco-queen clothes didn't help any. But his confidence and charisma rose above all the minor flaws to make him irresistible. And when he performed, he shone like a supernova.

Adder turned his radiant smile from the fans to Kalil. In one blinding second, Kalil knew his feelings for Adder had gone far beyond anything easy or safe.

He'd gone and fallen for the crazy asshole. He'd fallen in love, and what the fuck was he supposed to do now?

Tell him, an inner voice sounding suspiciously like Vi whispered. *Tell him how you feel. Either he feels the same way or he doesn't. And if he doesn't, isn't it better to find out now?*

Kalil gulped. Could he do it? Just sit Adder down and say, "Hey, dude, I'm in love with you"?

More to the point, could he keep it together if Adder didn't love him back?

He had no idea. But he thought maybe it was time to find out.

Chapter Twelve

Kalil had been acting odd ever since their post-performance bows. Nervous and distracted, yet quite clearly brimming with an elation he was unable to contain.

It bothered Adder in a way he couldn't quite pinpoint. After all, it wasn't that anything seemed *wrong,* exactly. In fact, the gleam in Kalil's eyes reminded Adder of a child who'd just received a pony for his birthday.

The problem was, the happy shine in those dark eyes hid a skulking *something* which suggested Kalil's inner child was rather frightened of ponies.

Adder made several attempts to get Kalil alone and ask him what was going on, but they all failed. First, everyone was busy breaking down the set. When they'd finished Kalil and Vi wanted to remain at the Gandhi stage for Library Fire's set. After that, Harpo claimed that since they were already there, they should stay and see Beck, his musical hero and man-crush (though he would wax off all his body hair before admitting the latter).

By the time Beck's set ended, night had fallen and everyone—Adder included—felt in the mood for a party. Jordan knew someone who was related to someone who'd once slept with someone else, and the entire band ended up with invitations to Beck's private after party. Thus, the Eastern sky had begun to pale by the time Adder and Kalil finally stumbled back to their hotel room.

"Oh my God," Kalil groaned, falling backward onto the bed. "I am so wiped."

"As am I." Adder plopped down beside Kalil and grinned at the ceiling. "But what a glorious way to wear oneself out."

"You got that right." Kalil laughed. "Shit, we were at a party with Beck. Fucking *Beck,* dude! Wow."

"Indeed." Adder turned to look at Kalil. "You were wonderful tonight, darling."

Kalil beamed. "*We* were wonderful."

Reaching sideways, Adder took Kalil's hand in his. "We were."

Silence fell and stretched on. Golden light edged the thick red curtains, growing stronger by the second. At first, Adder thought Kalil had fallen asleep. Then he noticed Kalil's fingers bunching the crimson and gold comforter, and the memory of his strange behavior earlier came rushing back.

Rolling onto his side, Adder propped himself up on one elbow and gazed down at Kalil's pensive expression with no small amount of worry. "Kalil?"

Kalil visibly shook himself and focused on Adder's face. "Yeah?"

"You've been a bit off all night. What's troubling you?"

Dropping his gaze, Kalil bit his lip. "I...I was thinking before that I...that, that I... Um..."

He trailed off, and Adder frowned. Kalil would seem calm enough to the uninformed, but Adder knew how his lover looked when on the edge of panic—the rapid pulse fluttering in his neck, the slightly too-wide eyes, the gray cast of his skin underneath his natural darkness.

Adder had no idea why Kalil was like this, now of all times, but every cell in his body longed to fix it. Leaning forward, he cupped Kalil's cheek in his free hand. "Tell me what's wrong, Kalil. I want to help, if I can."

Kalil's gaze met his. Fear, confusion and a bone-deep need shone from his eyes, and Adder's breath caught. For one soul-searing second, he felt as if he stood on the brink of a discovery that would change him forever. Then Kalil blinked and looked away, and the moment was gone.

"I... I was just thinking that, um, we should do this again." Kalil glanced at Adder, an anemic half-smile tilting up one corner of his mouth. "The tour, I mean. It was totally cool."

True though it may be, that hadn't been what Kalil was about to say before. Adder knew it as surely as he knew his own name. But whatever the real problem was, Kalil clearly wasn't ready to talk about it. Adder could respect that. He *would* respect that, even though he couldn't help feeling as if he'd just lost a once-in-a-lifetime chance. At what, he had no idea.

That, of course, was the problem. But he hadn't a clue how to coax Kalil into confiding in him.

Lacking any other choice in the matter, he forced a smile, for his lover's sake. "I agree one hundred percent, my dear. We should start planning our next tour soon, I think."

Kalil nodded, disappointment and relief clear as the brightening day in his expression. He reached up, wound both arms around Adder's neck and pulled him down for a slow, thorough kiss.

Adder opened up and let the inevitable desire rise inside him. When Kalil was ready to talk, Adder would be there for him. Right now, they were together in bed in a room where disturbance was much less likely than at home. Adder had every intention of enjoying it.

✧

It was strange how a mere nine days back in a familiar routine could make the most thrilling, exciting, perfectly brilliant month of one's life seem like a faded dream.

Sighing, Adder slumped onto the tattered old sofa in the studio lounge. He'd called a break from rehearsal just for a chance to be alone with his thoughts. The tour had been amazing, ending with their best performance to date at the TART Festival. Adder hadn't wanted it to end, and he couldn't help feeling a bit isolated because of that. Yes, the whole band had thoroughly enjoyed themselves and were eager to repeat the experience. Adder, however, literally hadn't cared to come home, unlike his bandmates. He liked Atlanta, but he thought he could live quite happily out of suitcases and hotel rooms if it meant being washed in the love of hundreds of people every single night. The feeling was addictive.

Kalil wandered in, plopped onto the couch and squeezed Adder's knee. "Hey."

As always, the mere sight of Kalil's face warmed Adder's heart, but he couldn't manage more than a faint smile. "Hello, K."

Cocking his head sideways, Kalil pinned Adder with a curious look. "Are you okay? You seem kind of down."

Adder shrugged. "A bit of post-tour letdown, I suppose."

"Oh. Yeah I can see that, I guess. The tour was fantastic." Kalil rested his head on Adder's shoulder. "I'm kind of glad to be home, though."

Adder gave a noncommittal hum. If Kalil was truly happy to be home, Adder hadn't seen much proof of it. The vague melancholy he'd sensed from Kalil the night of the TART show had faded somewhat in the intervening days, but hadn't gone away. Every time Adder asked him what was wrong, Kalil brushed him off and claimed it was nothing. After Kalil had nearly bitten his head off the other day for asking once again what was bothering him, Adder had started keeping his concern to himself.

He had not, however, stopped worrying. It bothered him to know that his lover was feeling troubled, but didn't see fit to share his problems with Adder.

"It *is* nice to be home," Adder said, even though it wasn't entirely true. He slipped his arm around Kalil's shoulders. "What say we go to Guero Bolero after practice this evening?"

Kalil turned to Adder with an excited sparkle in his eyes. "I think that sounds like a plan."

Laughing, Adder dragged Kalil onto his lap. The dear man absolutely adored the colorful bar's weekly Spanish Feast and Tango Night. "Do you know what I think, my darling?"

"Do I *want* to know?"

Adder smacked his thigh. "I think I deserve a kiss for my brilliant idea."

Kalil's smile turned wicked. "I think you're right."

Framing Adder's face between his palms, Kalil leaned in to brush his lips against Adder's. The touch was soft, chaste, and not at all what Adder had in mind. He swiped his tongue along Kalil's lower lip. Predictably, Kalil's mouth opened with the sweetest mewl in the universe. In a matter of seconds, the kiss went from innocent to indecent.

Naturally, that was when Jordan chose to enter the studio for the first time since they'd returned to Atlanta.

"Gather around, kids," she called, taking no notice of Kalil's surprised yelp. "I have big, big news."

Kalil slid off Adder's lap, his expression stormy. He grumbled something unintelligible under his breath, but it didn't seem to be aimed at Adder so he ignored it.

"What is it, Jordan?" Adder asked as Vi and Harpo piled in from the practice room.

Grinning, Jordan perched on the arm of the room's single chair. "I'll wait until you're all sitting down."

"Okay, *that's* a little nerve-wracking." Harpo plopped into the chair, looking apprehensive.

Vi dropped onto the sofa beside Kalil and grabbed his hand in hers. "We're sitting. What's up?"

Jordan's smile brightened. Her expression suggested that the excitement of her news filled her to near-bursting. Adder had never seen her like this. His pulse quickened in anticipation.

"Charles Reid called me today," Jordan said, finally. "He caught your set at the festival, and he wants to offer you kids a recording contract."

Adder reeled as if he'd been punched. *Oh, gods.*

"Charles Reid? You mean Vermillion Records' Charles Reid? *That* Charles Reid?" Harpo stared at Jordan, eyes wide and face ashen.

Jordan nodded. "The same, yes."

"Oh my *fucking* God," Vi breathed. "We're gonna record for Vermillion! Oh shit oh *shit*!"

Reaching across Kalil's body, Adder patted Vi's knee. "Calm down, love. We don't have the contract just yet."

She gave him a look which said she knew he wanted to leap up and whoop in triumph as much as she did. He grinned and winked at her.

"Mr. Reid would like to meet with all of you to discuss his offer." Reaching into her purse, Jordan pulled out a business card and handed it to Harpo. "His number's on the card. Could you all be at my office at four o'clock tomorrow afternoon?"

"Certainly." Adder didn't ask the others. He knew for a fact they were all free at the appointed time.

"Wait, hang on just a minute," Kalil spoke up for the first time since Jordan's arrival. "Shouldn't we give this a little thought first?"

Harpo gaped at him as if he'd just sprouted horns and a tail. "Think about *what*? Dude, this is Vermillion Records we're talking about."

"They just signed Me & My Gay Friends a couple of months ago," Vi added helpfully. "It's a good label."

Kalil shook his head. "Yeah, but—"

"My dear Kalil," Adder interrupted. "Let's at least hear Mr. Reid's offer, hm?"

Kalil aimed a deadly glare at Adder, who raised his eyebrows in silent challenge. Sometimes he wondered if Kalil had a mutant gene which forced him to be contrary for no other reason than sheer bloody-mindedness.

"Okay, yeah, you're right." Kalil hunched his shoulders and gave Jordan a sheepish smile. "Sorry, I guess I'm kind of leery of rushing into stuff like that."

Jordan nodded. "Understandable, and smart. Listen to what he has to say. Then the five of us will discuss it and hopefully come to a consensus." She pushed to her feet. "All right, children. I believe you've been working on some new songs, you mind if I listen in on your practice?"

"Of course we don't mind, love." Adder glanced around. Vi and Harpo both nodded. Kalil, he couldn't help noticing, did not. *Gods, I thought we were past this.* Keeping his expression carefully blank, Adder stood and reached for Kalil's hand. "Break is officially over, my dears. Come along. I'd like to give 'Josephina' one more run-through before we move on."

Kalil took Adder's hand and let himself be hauled to his feet. Adder wound his fingers through Kalil's as everyone filed into the practice room. A surreptitious sideways glance at Kalil told Adder that his lover was brooding about this contract offer. Hardly a surprise—Kalil wouldn't be Kalil if he wasn't brooding about something or other—but the attitude rankled. They had a recording contract offer on the table. This was what they'd been working so hard for all this time. The label was a relatively new one, true, but they'd already gained a reputation for producing some of the most cutting-edge music in the business. The bands they'd dropped along the way always cried foul, of course. In Adder's opinion, however, those bands never had the chops to make it in the first place.

That Kalil was worried about being fucked over by the label was obvious, but Adder couldn't understand *why.* He and his band possessed the talent and the drive to be one of the top indie acts in the country. Perhaps the entire world. Why didn't Kalil see that? Why couldn't he share Adder's confidence in the band?

Or in you.

Adder didn't like to think about why Kalil's lack of faith in him personally hurt more than anything else.

Inside the practice room, Kalil let go of Adder's hand and slipped both arms around his waist. "Adder?"

"Yes, darling?" Adder touched Kalil's cheek, alarmed by the sudden anguish in his expression. "Are you all right?"

Kalil chewed his lower lip in an endearingly childlike manner. "I'm sorry."

Adder blinked. "For what?"

"For always being such an ass." Kalil gazed up at Adder with misery in his eyes. "I don't want us to get screwed, you know?"

"Of course you don't. None of us want that." Smiling, Adder stroked the wild curls away from Kalil's face. "Never fear, my sweet. We have Jordan looking out for us now. She won't let that happen. And neither will I."

Kalil smiled and nodded, but Adder felt his body stiffen and saw the hardness behind his eyes.

Adder stifled a sigh. He'd done his best to reassure Kalil. Success required taking chances. At some point Kalil would have to come to terms with that fact. If he couldn't do that, perhaps his future with the band wasn't as certain as Adder had thought.

The mere idea of Kalil being out of the band made Adder's insides quake. The horror of it wasn't just that their music would be much poorer without Kalil as its foundation. No, the part that turned Adder's blood to ice water was the certainty that if Kalil was out of the band, he'd be out of Adder's life altogether. And Adder couldn't bear the thought of living without Kalil.

Just what *that* meant, Adder didn't like to contemplate.

Luckily, practicing new songs took a great deal of concentration. Adder threw himself into his work, and soon enough the uncomfortable fact of his feelings faded into the background. With any luck, he wouldn't be forced to confront them anytime soon.

As was usually the case with such things, the twenty-three hours and change between Jordan's announcement and the appointment with Charles Reid crawled by at a snail's pace, yet the meeting arrived before Adder was quite ready for it.

He tugged at his favorite red and yellow plaid tie, loosening the knot until he felt able to draw a full breath. "Kalil? What time is it?"

Kalil pulled up the sleeve of his indigo silk shirt to check his watch. "Three fifty-five."

Leaning sideways across Vi, Harpo patted Adder's shoulder. "Relax, man."

Adder shot Harpo a deadly glare, which Harpo ignored. Sighing, Adder took Kalil's hand and wove their fingers together. Kalil's palm was hot and damp, the muscles twitching in Adder's grip. Perversely, it calmed him to know that Kalil was anxious as well. Adder despised this uncharacteristic attack of nerves, but knowing he wasn't alone helped.

He glanced sideways. Vi wore a high-necked, form-fitting purple dress which showed off her figure and made her skin glow. If she weren't chewing her thumbnail, she would have looked very elegant. Harpo sat ramrod straight in his chair, which was the only outward evidence of nerves on his part. He looked older than usual in an emerald green suit with a black shirt and tie and a black fedora with a green band.

Adder shot a surreptitious look over his shoulder at the half-open door of Jordan's office. He and his bandmates had dragged extra chairs into the small room nearly fifteen minutes ago, and had been waiting in tense impatience ever since for Jordan to fetch their guest from the building's lobby. Adder thought he might expire from excessive worry if they didn't arrive soon.

As if in answer to his musings, he heard the door of

Jordan's loft open. Voices sounded from the outer room. Adder brushed a bit of lint from his new red trousers, frowning at the way his fingers trembled. *Mr. Reid is here because you and these wonderful people beside you are the best. Remember that.*

Jordan bustled through the door, a tall man with graying hair and a beautifully tailored charcoal suit behind her. Adder stood, still clinging to Kalil's hand. Kalil, Harpo and Vi rose to their feet as well.

Smiling, Jordan laid a hand on the man's shoulder. "Kids, this is Charles Reid. Charles, this is Adder, Kalil Sabatino, Violet McGill and Harpo Hall."

Mr. Reid reached over and shook each of their hands in turn. "It's very nice to meet you all. You blew me away at the TART Festival."

Adder let go of Kalil's hand to shake Mr. Reid's. "Thank you, Mr. Reid. We're all quite excited to meet you as well."

The man flashed a mouthful of expensive dental work. "I think you'll be even more excited by what I have to offer you."

"Let's all sit," Jordan suggested before Adder could say anything else.

Mr. Reid and Jordan settled into the chairs behind Jordan's desk. Adder and his bandmates resumed their previous positions. As soon as they'd sat, Kalil took Adder's hand once more. Adder got the distinct feeling that Kalil was seeking comfort rather than merely being possessive. He gave Kalil's fingers a squeeze and got a sweet smile in return.

Clearing his throat to dispel the sudden tightness, Adder faced the man who might well determine the course of their careers. "So, Mr. Reid. Let's talk."

Chapter Thirteen

By the time Mr. Reid left forty-five minutes later, Adder knew they'd found the break toward which they'd been working ever since he and Harpo had first decided to play together three years ago.

He shook the executive's hand and bid him farewell in a giddy daze. The contract was perfect. Absolutely perfect.

It sounded perfect, at least. They hadn't actually read it yet. Charles Reid had brought enough copies for Jordan and each of the band members to read at their leisure. But even though they hadn't read through it yet, Mr. Reid had gone over the main points with them, and it certainly sounded like an excellent contract. Adder had already decided he wanted to sign, and he had no doubt the rest of the band would as well. Surely even his dear, cautious Kalil couldn't find any cause for concern.

After she'd ushered Mr. Reid out, Jordan returned to the office and shut the door behind her. "So? What do you think?"

"I think I'm getting my pen out of my purse, 'cause I'm ready to sign right now." Vi beamed at Adder. "I don't have much experience with contracts, but this seemed like a really good one to me."

Harpo nodded. "We'll retain all the rights to our own music without even having to argue about it, which is pretty fucking awesome. Especially since so many people get screwed on that point with their first contract."

"I agree. It sounds excellent. Very little negotiation needed, if everything Mr. Reid told us is correct." *And now for the difficult part.* Steeling himself and hoping for the best, Adder twisted sideways in his chair and gave Kalil his most dazzling smile. "What do you think, darling?"

Kalil's brow furrowed. "I don't know."

Adder's frustrated sigh was nearly drowned out by the noises of protest from Harpo and Vi. "Kalil, my dear, I realize that you are a cautious man by nature. However, I fail to see what you could possibly find objectionable about the contract we've been offered."

"You mean this contract you haven't even read yet?" Kalil snorted. "Yeah, because record company executives are always just *so* honest."

"You know damn well we're not gonna sign anything until we're sure it's all good," Harpo growled. "What's your problem, K?"

Ignoring Vi's hissed admonition for Harpo to be a bit more sensitive, Adder watched Kalil's face. Kalil dropped his gaze, cheeks flushing red. "All I fucking said is 'I don't know', because unlike *some* people, I don't jump into things with both feet without even bothering to look where I'm jumping." He cut a withering look in Harpo's direction. "Asshole."

Harpo remained unmoved, if his expression was anything to go by. "Okay, Mom, why don't you explain what the problem is?"

Kalil's jaw twitched. "Vermillion has a reputation for dropping bands when they start slipping off the public radar even a little. You know that as well as I do. And he didn't say anything about any kind of guarantee or obligation on their part. Just a one-year initial contract with 'options' to renew. It sounds to me like they can just drop us any time, for any reason they want, and we can't do a damn thing about it."

"They only drop bands who aren't selling," Vi protested, voicing a part of what Adder had been thinking not long before. "That's only good business."

"They dropped Brass Balls in the middle of a fucking European tour. They had to play Oktoberfest shows and shit to scrape up enough money to fly home." Kalil raised his face to meet Adder's gaze. "I don't see why y'all think it's so fucking strange that I don't want that to happen to us."

The words were defiant, but those big dark eyes held a desperate plea. As if Adder's continued good opinion of him mattered more than anything else. Adder had no idea how to feel about that.

Jordan's calm, quiet voice dispelled the need for Adder to answer, for which he was grateful. "I understand your concern, Kalil, and it's always good to be careful." She leaned her elbows on the table. "Of course I'll go over the contract myself with a fine-tooth comb, and you all need to understand what all it says before you sign. Okay?"

Judging by the mulish expression on Kalil's face, it was far from okay, but he gave a single curt nod. "Fine."

"All right, then. You kids read it over, tonight if you get the chance. Meanwhile, I'll review it and get back to you with my recommendations. At that point I'll go over it line by line with all four of you, and we'll talk about any changes that *any* of us"—she shot a significant glance at Harpo—"believe need to be made."

"That sounds excellent to me." Adder tightened his grip on Kalil's hand and stood, tugging Kalil to his feet as well. "We'll leave you to it, then, love. Thank you."

"I'm your manager, hon. Taking care of you kids is what I do." She made a shooing motion with her hands. "Now go on, I need to tie up some loose ends before I start reading this thing. I'll come by the studio tomorrow and we'll talk."

They said their goodbyes and filed out of Jordan's office. Vi and Harpo were already chattering excitedly about the contract offer by the time they walked out onto the sidewalk. Glowering gray clouds had rolled in while they'd been inside, and the breeze smelled of the oncoming rain.

Letting go of Kalil's hand, Adder slipped an arm around his shoulders. "There's a storm coming."

"Uh-huh. So?"

Kalil's voice was flat and cold, but an undercurrent of fear ran through it. Fear of what, Adder had not the tiniest inkling. He wished he knew. He longed to soothe away the strange mingling of apprehension and anger radiating from the man by his side.

Adder leaned down to nuzzle Kalil's hair. "So, darling, a rainy evening is perfect for hiding in our room and doing gloriously depraved things to each other's bodies, wouldn't you say?"

To his relief, Kalil chuckled. His arm wound around Adder's waist. "Horny bastard."

"Only for you, my beautiful K," Adder whispered, half to himself. "Only for you."

The sweet little noise Kalil made went straight to Adder's heart. He clutched his lover close and ignored the voice in his head warning him to tread carefully or risk losing the best thing that had ever happened to him.

"Goddamn fucking *shit*!" Throwing his drumsticks on the floor, Kalil jumped to his feet and kicked the throne hard enough to send pain flaring through his toe. The stool clattered across the practice room floor. "That's it. I fucking give up."

Vi sighed and shook her head. Harpo threw both hands in the air. "What the fuck, man? You know this song backwards and forwards, why the hell can't you get it right?"

Kalil shot his friend a silent glare. He knew why he couldn't seem to concentrate on his drumming today, but he wasn't about to say it. Bad enough that he didn't have the balls to tell Adder he was in love with him. Worse still that he'd had the "tell Adder/don't tell Adder" fight with himself every single day since the festival. The way everyone—except, ironically, Jordan—had not only ignored the potential danger of signing with Vermillion, but had gotten angry with him for pointing it out, had pushed him beyond his ability to cope. Try as he might, he couldn't let go of his hurt and anger, and that on top of everything else was seriously fucking up his ability to play.

Setting his violin on its stand, Adder strode over and pulled Kalil into his arms. Kalil closed his eyes, tucked his head under Adder's chin and let the steady rise and fall of Adder's chest calm him. He wished he and Adder were back in bed. For a few hours last night, making love with Adder while the rain pattered against the window, he'd felt perfectly at peace. Then they'd left the relative sanctuary of their room for the studio, and all the tension of the previous day had come rushing back.

Kalil wished with all his heart that it would just go away. But that wasn't going to happen. Not until the whole thing with the contract was resolved, one way or another.

Adder rubbed Kalil's back in long, soothing strokes. He didn't say anything, and Kalil was pathetically glad of it. There was no way he could put his thoughts into words without it coming out all wrong and causing a spectacular fight, and he didn't want to fight. He had the sinking feeling his relationship with Adder teetered on the brink of destruction. One more blow-up might push it over the edge, and Kalil was pretty sure that would do him in.

After a few minutes of silence broken only by Harpo and Vi whispering together, Adder drew back and studied Kalil's face. "All right now, sweetheart?"

A warm glow settled inside Kalil's rib cage. God, he loved it when Adder looked at him like that. Like he was the whole world, if only for a few seconds.

Kalil managed a smile. "Yeah, I'm okay. Sorry. I've just been...kind of tense lately."

"That, my darling, is the understatement of the decade. But I suspect you'd rather not discuss that right now, so we will save it for another time." Adder planted a kiss on Kalil's forehead. "Shall we try 'Soulbound' once more?"

"Definitely." Rising on tiptoe, Kalil gave Adder a quick kiss on the lips before pulling out of his embrace. "Where're my drumsticks?"

"On the floor where you threw them, Princess," Vi said, fingering her keyboard.

Kalil gave her a dirty look. She blew him a kiss. Shaking his head, Kalil retrieved his drumsticks and dragged his throne back into position.

He was about to sit when the door opened and Jordan came striding in. "Can you kids join me in the lounge for a minute? I'm on my way to New York right now, but I've finished studying Vermillion's contract and I'd like to go over it with you real quick before I have to leave for the airport. Did any of you read it yet?"

"I did." Kalil ignored the way Vi and Harpo both groaned as they trudged into the lounge. "And Adder too. I thought you were going to go over it line by line with us."

Jordan's eyebrows went up. "I am, just not right now. This meeting in New York is kind of last minute, but I can't put it off. So, what I'm going to do this afternoon is explain the major strengths and weaknesses of the contract, and the changes I'd recommend making. I'll be out of town for a couple of days, maybe longer but probably not. Anyone who hasn't read your copy of the contract yet, do it while I'm gone. I'll call you when I get back, and we can all sit down with it together. Sound good?"

Harpo, Vi and Adder all nodded their agreement. Kalil didn't feel as reassured as he was probably supposed to, but he clamped his mouth firmly shut and nodded as well. After all, it wasn't like Jordan expected them to make a decision before she'd had the chance to thoroughly explain everything and let them ask questions and make suggestions of their own. The fact that he was the only one likely to question anything at all was kind of beside the point.

Jordan settled herself onto the huge zebra-striped ottoman Vi had bought last weekend at the new thrift store in Little Five Points. Everyone else crowded onto the sofa. Kalil found himself squished sideways between Adder's bony hip and the arm of the couch. He wriggled until Adder scooted over enough for him to actually sit.

"Okay. So, basically, the contract is a good one." Opening her briefcase, Jordan took out four pieces of paper and handed one to each of them. "I've typed out the high points for you. The royalty rate is good. You're locked into a minimum of ten and a maximum of fifteen masters over a period of one year. Those numbers are negotiable."

Adder rubbed his chin. "That sounds reasonable to me.

Enough to produce a good, solid album without keeping us in the studio forever."

"What about the rights?" Vi asked. "Did he tell the truth about that?"

Jordan nodded. "The contract specifies that you will own the copyright to each song. Vermillion gets exclusive publication rights for the duration of the contract, but if the contract expires they lose exclusive publication rights even for their own masters. It's a little more complex than that, but that's the gist of it. From what I've been able to learn about Vermillion, this is standard for their contracts. And yes, it's very different from how anyone else in the business does things."

"What about the options thing?" Kalil asked, ignoring the triumphant smirk Harpo shot him. "It looked to me like they could pretty much refuse to renew the contract for any reason and they wouldn't even have to tell us why."

"Well, it's not as bad as all that, but you're essentially right. Contract renewal after the initial one-year term is at Vermillion's sole discretion." Jordan laid a hand on Kalil's knee before he could answer. "But that's still pretty standard in this business. We can probably renegotiate for something more solid later on, if you guys hit as big as I think you will, but you're not going to do better than that on your first contract. No company in the world is going to risk tying themselves to unproven talent."

If that was true, it only made Kalil more leery of the whole thing. Leaning back against the cushions, he frowned at the torn place on the right thigh of his jeans. This was going to end up being trouble for them. He could feel it in his bones. But there was no way Adder would listen to him as long as his precious Jordan kept telling them how fantastic the fucking contract was. And if Adder didn't listen, Harpo and Vi were a lost cause.

"I'm going to ask for a larger advance," Jordan continued, either oblivious to Kalil's discouragement or ignoring it. Kalil was betting on the latter. "And a higher royalty rate. You're new, so you won't get what I'm going to ask for, but you'll probably end up with higher than what's already on the table because this guy is *dying* to sign you. He didn't say that in so many words, of course, but I can tell. And, Adder, I'm going to have them add another three percent if you still insist on doing the production yourself."

"I do indeed." Adder's hand slid onto Kalil's knee and gave it a squeeze. "Are there any other changes you think need to be made?"

"Nothing major. There are a few things, they're spelled out on the sheet I gave you." Jordan glanced at her watch. "Shit, I need to run. Sorry to do this to you, guys, but duty calls." She stood, briefcase in hand, and gave them a smile. "Read through the contract, and the list I just gave you. Write down any questions you have, and any suggestions you have for changes, and I'll talk to you in a couple of days."

Adder stood to usher Jordan out. Kalil stayed put, staring at the piece of paper in his hands so he wouldn't have to look at Harpo or Vi. Much as he hated to admit it, they'd both become nearly as important to him as Adder, and it hurt to see them glaring at him like he'd done something unforgivable.

Harpo stood and walked over to the bar. "I'm getting a juice, y'all want anything?"

"I'll get my own." Pushing off the sofa, Vi sauntered over to join Harpo.

When the two of them put their heads together and started talking too low for him to hear, Kalil got up, set his paper on the ottoman and stalked back into the practice room. He parked himself at his drum kit and tapped out random rhythms with his sticks in an attempt to stop dwelling on all the horrible things that could happen if they signed a bad contract.

It didn't work. Visions of the various ways they could get screwed over drowned out every other thought.

Adder's arrival not long after was a relief. Kalil set his drumsticks down and walked over to meet Adder in the middle of the room. They stared at each other in silence for a moment. Kalil felt tongue-tied and uncomfortable, something which hadn't happened in Adder's company for months. It made him sad to feel that way.

"Why are you fighting this contract so hard?" Adder asked finally.

"You read it. You know what's wrong with it."

"Darling, you heard what Jordan said. The renewal option at the company's discretion is standard."

"So, just because it's standard operating bullshit, that means we have to just bend over and take it?"

An angry flush crept up Adder's neck and into his face. "You're creating monsters out of nothing. The only possible reason they could have for dropping us would be if we didn't sell. And you know as well as I do that will *not* happen."

Kalil let out a bitter laugh. "Just because we're a great band doesn't mean everybody's gonna love us. What if we don't hit right out of the gate, huh? If that happens, Charles Reid and his company will drop us like a fucking bad habit."

Adder's lips thinned. "You don't know that."

"I know it's happened to plenty of other bands." Taking a step forward, Kalil poked Adder in the chest. "If you don't think it can happen to us, you're kidding yourself."

Adder caught Kalil's wrist in a grip so tight it was painful. "I am not stupid, contrary to what you evidently believe. I know what could happen to us if things go wrong. But this is a huge opportunity for us. One we may never get again. I think that's worth the risk."

"All I'm saying—all I've said all along—is that we should be careful. We should ask for some kind of guarantee from them." Grimacing, Kalil twisted his hand. "Let go."

Adder didn't. Instead, he snagged Kalil's other wrist and gave them both a shake. "Listen to me," he hissed. "I. *Want.* This. Contract. And I will *have* it. Do you understand me?"

Shocked, Kalil stared into Adder's angry face. His eyes glittered, hard and cold as frost on the grass. Dread twisted deep in Kalil's gut. He hadn't wanted to fight, hadn't meant to, but here he was, with no good options left. Either he could shut up and lose all respect for himself, or he could stick to his guns and run the risk of losing Adder. It felt like riding a runaway truck off the edge of a mountain—no matter how he landed, it was going to hurt.

"I'm not trying to keep us from getting a contract. I want one too." Kalil licked his lips, wishing his voice wouldn't wobble so much. "I just don't want us to get fucked over."

"We won't get fucked over."

"You don't know that."

"I *do* know that! We have Jordan now. She'll take care of us."

Adder's blind faith in Jordan made Kalil's head hurt. He ground his teeth together. "Dammit, Adder, I know you think she hung the fucking moon, but she doesn't have some kind of magical fairy power to keep away evil, and she does not know everything. I just think—"

"I know what you think, my *darling* Kalil." Adder spat the name like it was a piece of rotten meat. "You still think, after all this time, after all I've tried to convince you otherwise, that she and I are having an affair. Well, I'm fucking *sick* of trying to make you see that we aren't."

Kalil's stomach dropped into his feet. He hadn't thought any such thing in ages, and had no idea why Adder would believe he had. "I…I don't—"

"Shut up." Adder's fingers dug into Kalil's wrists so hard his hands started going numb. "I know what else you think. You *think* you know more than Jordan about the music business, and about what should and should not be in a contract. Well, you *don't*."

Fed up, Kalil twisted and yanked his arms from Adder's grip. "If my opinion's so fucking unimportant, maybe I should just leave."

"Maybe you should."

Three quietly spoken words had never sounded so loud before. Kalil hunched forward, feeling like he'd been kicked in the chest. In the back of his mind, he'd always figured it would end this way. That he'd be thrown over in favor of Adder's ambitions. But fuck, it hurt more than he ever thought it could.

When he thought he could breathe again, Kalil forced himself to stand up straight. "Fine. I will."

It took everything Kalil had to walk out the door, but he did it. He kept his gaze fixed on the floor. If he looked at Adder, he'd collapse into a sobbing heap, and there was no fucking way he was giving the bastard the satisfaction of watching him fall apart.

Harp and Vi both called to him as he slunk through the lounge with his head down. They both sounded worried, but Kalil didn't stop to reassure them. What was the point? Everything was blown to hell now. Nothing either of them said could possibly make any difference.

Kalil made it almost three blocks before his legs gave out on him. He sat hard on the sidewalk between a leather bar and a sandwich shop, ignoring the sea of people flowing around him.

He was out. Out of the band, out of Adder's life, and God, he'd never felt so desolate. Cradling his head in both hands, he shut his eyes and wondered if he'd ever have a reason to get up again.

After the fourth passerby crouched to ask him if he was all right, he forced himself to his feet. He didn't know how long the rest of the band would practice without him, but knew he wanted to be gone before they got home. If he saw or spoke to Adder again right now, he'd either beg for another chance like a pathetic idiot, or punch the smug asshole in the face. Neither was an acceptable option. He needed to go home, get his things and get the hell out of Dodge. Now.

Pulling his cell phone out of his pocket, he dialed his brother's place. "Tony? Yeah, hi. I need your help."

Kalil's precipitous departure brought rehearsal to a grinding halt.

They tried to continue, using their trusty old drum machine. Surely, Adder reasoned, it would be sufficient for a couple of hours. But they only made it through five songs before it became painfully apparent that Adder was far too upset to continue. Once Vi finally pried the sordid tale of Kalil's departure from him, Adder allowed himself to be led into the lounge and plunked onto the sofa between his two friends.

"I was terrible to him." Adder slumped until he could rest his head against the back of the couch. "He needed me to listen to him, but instead of listening I told him my desire to sign this contract was more important to me than him."

Taking his hand, Vi squeezed his fingers. "Come on, Adder, I know you. I don't believe you said any such thing."

"Not in so many words, no. But that is precisely what I led him to believe." Adder let out a deep sigh. "I am such an ass when I'm angry."

Harpo snorted. "You got that right."

Vi reached across Adder to smack Harpo's shoulder. "Would you have a little sensitivity, please? God."

Harpo held up both hands in a gesture of capitulation. Vi shot him a dark look. "Anyway, Adder, I'm sure he'll come around. You know how he is, he gets mad and sulks for a while, then he gets over it."

"I know. I hope you're right." Adder summoned an anemic smile for Vi. "The moment we get home, I'm going to talk to him. I'm going to get down on one knee and beg his forgiveness for being so horrible to him."

"You told him to leave, asshole. He won't be there." Harpo shook his head. "God, I can't believe you did that. Where the fuck are we gonna get another drummer that good? I could fucking kill you right now."

"I wasn't suggesting he leave the band. Or me, for that matter. I simply thought it would be a good idea if he left the studio. Both of us needed time to calm down, and..." A terrible thought struck Adder like a hammer to the head. He fixed Harpo with a wide-eyed stare. "Oh gods. You don't really think he would...?"

"Would what? Get pissed off, completely misunderstand every word out of your mouth and run away like the hotheaded idiot he is?" Harpo rolled his eyes. "Sorry, I was under the impression that you'd been living with him for almost a year.

My mistake."

Adder couldn't answer. He felt as if all the air had been sucked out of his lungs. What if Harpo was right? What if Kalil was really gone? Gone from the band, and gone from Adder's life?

"He can't be," Adder whispered. "He can't."

"Well, he just might be. Good job, Adder." With a pat to Adder's knee, Harpo pushed to his feet. "Well. I don't know about you two, but I'm going home. If Kalil's still there, maybe I can talk him into staying. Of course he's even more stubborn than A-hole here, so who knows."

The thought of facing Kalil right now made Adder's knees shake with equal parts terror and longing. Letting go of Vi's hand, Adder stood, picked up his satchel and slung it over his shoulder. "Very well. Let's go."

Harpo eyed him with caution as Vi ran to get her purse from behind the bar. "You sure this is a good idea? He might not be too happy to see you right now."

Adder's pride told him to declare that the fault wasn't entirely his, that Kalil certainly bore his share of the blame for what had happened. A larger part, however, realized that getting Kalil back was far more important than being right. Especially when Adder knew he himself was as much in the wrong as Kalil.

"All right, guys, I'm driving." Vi fished the keys out of her bag as they all trooped down the hallway to the front door. "And, if Kalil's there, I think I should do the talking too."

"But—"

Vi stopped Adder's words with a look. "Adder, I love you, but you've already hurt Kalil pretty bad, and you say some phenomenally stupid things when you're upset. Harpo, you're not any better, so just don't even start."

"I didn't even say anything," Harpo protested.

"Not yet, but you were about to." Vi pointed a stern finger at Harpo. "I don't want either one of you saying another word to Kalil until I get to talk to him. Are we clear?"

Wrinkling his nose, Harpo opened the front door and held it so Vi and Adder could walk through. "Yes, Mommy Dearest."

Adder interrupted before relations between Harpo and Vi devolved into a full-blown fistfight. "Vi? Do you really think I hurt him with what I said?"

"Obviously you did. He's nuts about you. As important as the band and his music are to him, I think you're even more important. So, yeah, you telling him he ought to leave probably made him feel like shit. Especially right on top of us all more or less brushing off what he had to say about the contract." She sighed as she slid her sunglasses on. "I just hope he hasn't gone for good. I hate to see you hurting too."

Adder ignored that last statement. It was bad enough that Vi evidently knew how much Kalil leaving would tear Adder apart. The reasons behind that truth were ones Adder couldn't bring himself to consider too closely. Especially now.

The three of them climbed into the van in a heavy, apprehensive silence. Adder knew Vi and Harpo were thinking of what would happen if they had just lost their drummer. Would Vermillion still want them? Would they ever be able to find anyone with a quarter of Kalil's talent and creativity?

The same worry hovered in the back of Adder's brain, but the fear of losing Kalil as his lover loomed like a shadow over everything else. He tried to imagine waking up every day without Kalil's warm, solid body in his arms, and the vision made him shake all over. He rested his head against the glass of the passenger-side window and shut his eyes.

The short ride back home seemed to last eons. When Vi

finally parked the van in the garage beneath the building, Adder jumped out and took the stairs two at a time. He ignored Vi's indignant squawking. No matter what his friends said, he was determined to be the first one to talk to Kalil.

If he was even there, of course. The possibility that he might not be was a very real one.

At the top of the stairs, Adder pulled his keys from his satchel. The key ring fell from his hand. Cursing under his breath, he bent, snatched it up and shoved the key into the lock before his trembling fingers could fumble again.

He pushed the door open and rushed in just as Harpo and Vi caught up with him. "Kalil! Are you here?"

The silence echoed his words back to him. Heart in his throat, Adder ran down the short hallway to the bedrooms. "Kalil?" *Gods, please be here. Please.*

Their bedroom was as empty as the rest of the place. Worse, all Kalil's things had been taken.

Adder sat on the edge of the bed, feeling numb. Kalil was gone. Really, truly gone. He'd left, over a stupid fight.

"I called his cell," Harpo announced, walking into the room and sitting beside Adder. "He's not answering."

Adder swallowed hard. "He can't leave the band. If he doesn't wish to...to be with me any longer, I can understand that." *No, no I can't. Why did he leave me? I thought we were stronger than this.* "But surely he wouldn't leave the band."

"You ought to know him better than that by now." Harpo let out a defeated sigh. "Well, I left a voice mail for him. I told him we were sorry for being dicks and that we needed him in the band."

Adder kept his gaze fixed on his clasped hands. His hair fell forward enough to veil his face, and he was glad of it. He didn't want Harpo to see the tears gathering in his eyes. Adder did not cry. Ever. It infuriated him that Kalil could make him this emotional with nothing but his absence.

Vi wandered in and leaned against the wall beside the door. "His drum kit's still at the studio. He won't leave that behind. He'll have to come back for it. Even if he won't talk to us on the phone, he can't avoid it when he comes back to get his drums."

A sliver of hope cut through the gloom in Adder's heart. "That's true. Kalil loves his drums. He'll come back for them, and we'll convince him to come back to us." Lifting his face, he gave Vi a faint smile. "Well. It seems we are at loose ends until our dear Kalil decides to talk to us. What shall we do?"

"We still need to read through that contract," Vi mused, twisting a bit of her gauzy red skirt between her fingers. "Why don't we do that? We can read it together, and write down our questions and stuff."

"Yeah. Maybe we can find something in it that'll convince Special K it's not as big a risk as he thinks." Harpo stood and clapped Adder on the shoulder. "Come on, Adder. Reviewing the contract'll keep us busy until Kalil calls back."

Adder did not want to read the contract. In fact, the very thought of it made him sick to his stomach. But he knew Harpo was right. Kalil would have to at least call sometime in the next day or two, if only to get his drums back, and Adder desperately needed something to tame his runaway thoughts in the meantime. If he could only suppress his current emotional reactions, concentrating on this bit of business would do the trick.

His mind made up, Adder rose to his feet. "Very well. I have my copy in my satchel. I'll read aloud, shall I?"

Harpo and Vi both agreed, and the three of them filed into the combination living and dining room. Adder fetched his copy of the contract, Jordan's bullet list, extra paper and pens, and the three of them gathered at the table.

Adder began reading with a sense of relief. With mouth and brain both usefully occupied, maybe he could stop kicking himself for driving away the person he'd only just realized was more important to him than anything else.

Chapter Fourteen

Kalil didn't call, and he didn't return for his drum kit. Adder arrived at the studio at an unprecedented ten a.m. the day after Kalil left, only to find the drums gone and a note from Anthony Sabatino on the practice room door threatening bodily harm to Adder for hurting his little brother.

In spite of his by-now-desperate need to see Kalil and apologize to him, Adder couldn't help being relieved that he hadn't been there when Tony arrived to fetch Kalil's drums. Adder had met K's older brother. He did not relish being on the man's bad side.

Adder tried to hold on to his hope that Kalil would eventually come around. But as the days passed with no word from Kalil and no answer to his frequent calls, Adder began to realize that it was over. Kalil was gone, and he wasn't coming back.

The knowledge sent Adder spiraling into an abyss of black despair. He couldn't even summon the energy to be angry at Kalil for deserting him and the band so thoroughly. Music provided him with a reason to get up in the morning—or, more frequently, the afternoon—else he never would have left his bed. He only stopped spending all his extra time there when Vi washed the sheets and they no longer smelled like sex and Kalil.

Jordan's negotiations with Vermillion over their contract took almost a month. By the time they all gathered in Jordan's office to sign, Adder had sequestered his grief behind a steel wall of determination. He had to get on with his life. At the moment he was only going through the motions, but he knew that wouldn't last forever. Eventually, he would get over his loss and begin enjoying life again. In the meantime, he had obligations to fulfill, and his love for creating and performing music remained undimmed.

He would survive this. He would not allow himself to entertain any other outcome.

Unfortunately, surviving the loss of Kalil on a professional level proved to be somewhat more difficult, for reasons over which Adder had no control. All the resolve in the world couldn't summon a talented drummer out of thin air. By the last week of August they still hadn't found anyone to replace Kalil. With their reserved recording time for their first album coming up in mid-September, Adder reluctantly agreed to work with session drummers until they could find a new permanent addition to the band.

"It won't be so bad," Harpo reassured him three weeks later, as the two of them followed Vi into the lobby of Vermillion's posh studio in the heart of Atlanta's business district. "Vermillion's got some fantastic musicians playing session for them. I know they won't be the same as Kalil—"

"They won't be as *good* as Kalil." Adder glanced around. The place practically screamed wealth, with its overabundance of expensive wood and marble and all the gold records on the walls. "No one is as good as Kalil."

Harpo sighed. "Yeah. He was perfect, huh?"

A giant vise squeezed Adder's ribs. He nodded, not trusting himself to speak. After more than two months, the pain of

Kalil's departure hadn't eased one iota. Adder sometimes wondered if it ever would.

Somewhere in the back of his mind, he knew why this breakup had left him so heartsick. But admitting it to himself at this point would change nothing. So he ignored it, and tried to pretend Kalil had been nothing to him but a casual lover.

Slowing her pacc, Vi dropped back to walk beside Adder. She took his hand, weaving their fingers together. Adder kissed the top of her head. He didn't think he would have made it through the past few weeks without her silent support. She never said a word, but he got the distinct impression that she knew exactly what he was feeling. It helped to have someone with whom to share the burden of his unspoken feelings, even if that sharing was achieved without words.

A frighteningly thin young woman met them at the door leading from the lobby to the innards of the studio. She smiled and held out a hand covered in rings. "Adder, Vi and Harpo, right? I'm Candace Shores, I'll be your assistant while you're recording with us."

"It's nice to meet you, Candace." Adder shook her hand, then stepped back to let Harpo and Vi do the same. "We're all very excited about recording with Vermillion."

Candace gave him a strange look, which he ignored. He knew he didn't seem particularly excited. In fact, Harpo had assured him repeatedly that he barely seemed alive, never mind excited about anything. But he was doing the best he could, and he refused to be bothered by the fact that everyone he encountered these days looked at him with cautious pity.

With a quick glance in Adder's direction, Vi stepped up and hooked her arm through Candace's. "Let's go back to the booth, Candace. I can't wait to meet the tech team and get started."

A lovely pink blush stained Candace's pallid cheeks, and

Adder grinned in spite of himself. If Vi had any sexual interest in other women, she'd have them lining up outside her bedroom door, and Adder was betting Candace would be at the head of the queue.

Thanking his lucky stars for Vi's ability to draw attention to her and thus away from him, Adder trailed the rest of the group through the doorway and down a long hallway carpeted in plush midnight blue. Up until Kalil left, Adder had always craved the spotlight both on and off stage. Now, he just wanted to be invisible. He rather resented Kalil for that.

At the end of the hall, Candace opened a door on their left and led them into a small room done in shades of pale gray and dark red. A long, low sofa and two chairs sat against the back wall. Two middle-aged men occupied seats in front of a state-of-the-art sound board. They both acknowledged the band's entrance with a distracted nod as they fiddled with the equipment.

Adder walked in, gazing around with as much interest as he could muster. A huge window behind the sound board looked out on a large recording booth. Their instruments, mics and four sets of headphones lay in wait for them. A stocky young man with close-cropped brown hair and a straggly beard sat at the drum kit, tapping on the cymbals.

"This is Quentin James and Brian Overton, your engineers," Candace said, indicating the men at the sound board. "Your session drummer's Joe Taylor. He's a terrific drummer and great to work with, plus he's been listening to your stuff and working on the drum parts. I think you'll all get along just fine."

I doubt that. Steeling himself, Adder straightened his shoulders and marched into the booth. He held out his hand. "Hello. I'm Adder. This is Violet McGill and Harpo Hall. I believe we'll be working together."

Setting down his drumsticks, Joe walked over with his hand out and a wide, easy smile on his face. "Hey there, Adder. I'm..." *not Kalil* "...Joe. I've heard a lot about y'all. I'm looking forward to working with you."

"As are we." Adder shook Joe's hand and forced himself to smile. "So. Shall we get started?"

As everyone scurried around, Adder stood at the mic with his head bowed to hide the anguish he couldn't keep from his eyes. He'd never missed Kalil more than he did at this moment. It felt utterly wrong to begin their first album without Kalil at the drums.

Ever since that horrible June afternoon, Adder had lived with a near-crippling regret for the things he'd said. Worse yet was the regret for the one thing he hadn't said.

Not that it would have made any difference if he'd recognized his own feelings in time to tell Kalil he loved him. Surely Kalil never would have left if he felt the same.

"Adder?" Vi touched his arm. "We're ready."

For a second, Adder didn't think he could do it. But there was more at stake here than his shattered heart, and these people were counting on him.

Shoving his sorrow back behind its wall, Adder lifted his head and met Vi's worried gaze. "Very well, my dears. Let's begin."

"Thank you, Atlanta! Good night!"

Half hidden behind his drums, Kalil set down his sticks and stretched while Bucket War's singer attempted to rouse a little post-show enthusiasm from the sparse audience. Kalil didn't hold out much hope for success. Spike was a good singer, but he just didn't have the knack for engaging people.

Not like Adder does.

As always, the thought of Adder sent a stab of pain through Kalil's gut. Scowling, he stood and started breaking down his drums. After four months, he shouldn't still feel this devastated every time he remembered Adder's voice, or his smile, or the way he would play with Kalil's hair when they were lying in bed together.

Too bad his stupid heart didn't give a shit about how he *should* feel. It decided to drag him through his own personal hell every time his mind turned to Adder. Which was way too often for Kalil's comfort.

The lights came up while Kalil was taking down the cymbals. He could hear Spike and the rest of the band talking, but had no desire to join in. This was just a temporary gig. The band's regular drummer was laid up with a broken arm. Kalil had agreed to fill in for her because Bucket War was the house band five nights a week at Scandalous, and therefore got paid a regular and predictable amount. Drumming tepid pop rhythms for a room full of apathetic yuppies didn't feed his soul the way playing with Adder, Vi and Harpo had, but it meant cash in his pocket every Thursday, and he needed the money right now.

Besides, he was never again going to find what he'd had with Adder. Not in music, and not in life. He hated how much that made him want to just curl up and die.

He didn't look up when he heard footsteps coming across the stage toward him. If it was a fan—not that this band had very many—they'd only want to know where to find Spike, and Kalil thought he might hit the next person who asked him that. Since beating up groupie wannabes would probably get him fired, he chose to ignore them. If it was someone besides a fan...well, who else would it be? It wasn't like Adder was going to come to this bland, shiny place, confess his undying love for Kalil and carry him off into the sunset, no matter what Kalil's persistent fantasies wanted to think.

"Hi, Kalil."

Vi. Oh my God. Kalil froze, his heart racing. If Vi was here, there could only be one reason for it. She was going to try and talk him into coming back.

Shit.

With great reluctance, he raised his head. Sure enough, Vi stood there watching him with a wistful smile on her face. "Vi. Um. Hey. What're you doing here?"

"I just wanted to see you. I miss you, K." She let out a soft, sad little laugh. "Shit, come here."

Before Kalil quite knew what was happening, he had an armful of sobbing female. Ignoring the strange looks they got from his bandmates and the bar crew, he held Vi tight, rubbed her back and murmured, "It's okay, it's okay," in her ear, even though he had no idea what was wrong, never mind whether or not it would actually be okay. A lump rose in his throat. He'd missed Vi and Harpo almost as much as he missed that big green-haired jackass, and he couldn't deny that he was happy to see Vi again.

Now if only he could get her to stop crying.

After a while, the sobs trailed off into sniffles and hiccups. Vi drew back, wiping her eyes. "Sorry. I swear I didn't come here just to cry on you."

"*Just* to cry on me? So you admit the crying was part of your evil plan?" He raised his eyebrows in question.

She giggled, and Kalil smiled. He'd always hated to see Vi

sad or upset. Joking around never failed to cheer her up.

"It was a last-minute addition to the plan." She took both his hands in hers and gazed at him with a solemn expression. "Actually, I came to talk to you. Is there somewhere we can go?"

Kalil's stomach rolled. He thought he could guess what the topic of discussion would be, and it scared the crap out of him. Ignoring the increasingly desperate phone calls from Vi, Harpo and even Jordan begging him to come back had been easy. Much easier than ignoring Adder's calls. They'd stopped almost three months ago. But he knew he'd never be able to say no to Vi's sweet, pleading face. Which was probably why they sent her.

"Did A...did he tell you to come?" Maybe it was a dumb thing to ask, but he had to do it. At least Vi would tell him the truth.

"No, he didn't. No one knows I came here tonight. I just..." She made a frustrated noise. "Look, I know you think you've moved on, from Adder and from us. But Adder hasn't. And now that I've seen you, I can tell you haven't either. You're both just...fucking *pining,* and it's ridiculous." She gave his hands a gentle shake. "K, please come back. Please. We need you. Adder's fired five drummers already. No one fits us like you do."

Gratifying as it was to hear that, it wasn't the one thing Kalil needed to convince him. How in the hell could he go back and work with Adder every day, when he loved the bastard so much it hurt and he knew Adder didn't—wouldn't ever—feel the same? He couldn't. Cowardly? Maybe. But still true.

"Vi, I'm sorry, I—" His brain registered what else she'd said, and he frowned. "Wait, what? What do you mean, Adder hasn't moved on? And I'm not pining."

"Yes you are." She let go of his left hand and stopped his protests with a finger against his lips. "Even if you aren't, Adder is. He's not the same person he was before you left. He thinks he's got everyone fooled, but he doesn't. Even his performances are slipping. That *has* to tell you something, right?"

It did. No matter what else happened, no matter what was going on in Adder's life, he'd never let it affect his performances before. It would take something truly monumental to take the sparkle from Adder's stage presence.

Perversely, that fact gave Kalil more hope than he'd had in months. If his leaving could affect Adder so profoundly, maybe his feelings for Kalil were stronger than either of them had realized. And if that was the case, maybe there was a future for them after all.

There was just one other thing he needed to know. "I heard y'all signed with Vermillion. Is that true?"

Vi nodded. "Yeah. We're in the studio right now."

"Recording. That's...that's great." He drew a shaky breath. "So. How's the contract? I know Jordan would've fought for whatever she could get."

"She did. We got a really good royalty rate, and a nice advance for the album." Vi bit her lip. "It's a really good contract, Kalil. I know you're worried about them dropping us, but I honestly don't think that's going to happen. Besides, you have to take a risk to get anywhere in this business. You know that."

Adder had said pretty much the same thing the day Kalil left. He'd thought about it a lot since then and come to realize that Adder and Vi were both right. If he ever wanted to make it, he had to stick his neck out at some point.

The big problem now would be learning to work with Adder whether they were together or not.

"I'll think about it," Kalil whispered.

That was as much as he could promise, but it seemed to be enough for Vi. She smiled. "You do that." Leaning forward, she kissed his cheek, then let go of his hand. "Don't be a stranger, huh?"

Kalil watched as she turned and walked out of the bar. Part of him longed to go with her, but he fought it. He wasn't doing a damn thing without thinking it through first.

Bucket War's bassist, Annie, sidled up to him. "Who was that girl?"

Kalil shrugged. "An old friend."

"Looked like more than that to me." Annie's eyes went wide. "Oh shit, that was Violet McGill, she plays keyboards for Adder! Wow." She glanced toward the door of the bar, then turned back to Kalil with a thoughtful look. "Didn't you used to play for them?"

Kalil's chest constricted. "Yeah."

"Huh. Too bad it didn't work out." She patted his shoulder. "Good deal for us, though."

"Yeah."

Silence fell. Kalil went back to breaking down his kit so he wouldn't have to look Annie in the eye. After a while, she wandered away, and Kalil sagged in sheer relief. These people could never truly be his friends. All they knew about him was that he was gay, and the only reason they knew that was because everyone in the city knew he and Adder had once been a couple. They didn't know him, because he kept his distance, as he had with every band he'd sat in on since June.

He hadn't realized it before Vi brought it up, but he was lonely. How could he be here? He should be with Adder, Vi and Harpo. It was where he belonged.

Shit. I'm actually thinking of going back.

For the first time, he found the idea attractive instead of just terrifying.

It took Kalil three days to work up the courage to go to Adder's practice studio. He tried to tell himself he was pondering the pros and cons of returning, but he knew damn well that wasn't true. Every time he imagined himself walking into that building and seeing Adder again, his pulse raced and his knees knocked together.

He was scared shitless, and that was the bald truth.

Irritation and disgust with himself eventually shoved him into action. Which was how he found himself standing in a familiar alley on a Thursday afternoon, staring at a familiar door which led to a studio where he'd spent some of the best times of his life.

There's still time to back out, the shameless coward in his head informed him. *No one knows you're here. You could leave right now, and go back to how you were.*

The problem was, he'd come to hate his life without Adder and the band. Living with his brother and sister-in-law wasn't so bad, but the rest of his existence had become rote and dull. The thought of going back to that wasn't scary. It was depressing. At this point, he kind of preferred scary.

Straightening his shoulders, he pounded on the door, then stepped back to wait. He hoped someone answered soon, before his courage deserted him.

When the door cracked open, Kalil had an endless second to imagine Adder opening the door, seeing Kalil and sweeping him into his arms, whispering "I love you" and kissing him like both their lives depended on it. He didn't know whether to be relieved or disappointed when the door swung wide to reveal Harpo on the other side.

"Special K!" Launching himself at Kalil, Harpo hugged him hard enough to squeeze all the breath from his lungs. "Goddamn, it's good to see you, man."

"You too." Kalil felt a smile tugging at his mouth as he returned Harpo's hug. "I've missed y'all."

"We've missed you like you would not fucking believe." Harpo drew back, his expression hopeful. "Are you coming back?"

Kalil's mouth went bone dry, but he nodded. "If you'll have me."

A huge grin lit up Harpo's face like a thousand-watt bulb. "Fuck yeah, we'll have you. Are you kidding me?" Slinging an arm around Kalil's neck, Harpo pulled him inside and kicked the door shut. "Just wait 'til Adder and Vi see you. They're gonna shit. None of us even knew where you were, dude."

Somehow, it didn't surprise Kalil at all to know Vi hadn't told anyone about her visit. *I just hope she was right, and Adder actually does want me back.*

They breezed down the hallway and through the lounge—which was as ugly as ever, Kalil noted fondly—and reached the practice room door before Kalil was ready. He could hear Adder's voice. He started to shake.

"Hey guys," Harpo called as he pulled Kalil into the room. "Look who I found hanging around outside."

The room went dead quiet. After a silence that seemed to stretch on forever, Vi bounded up and hugged him hard, telling him how much she'd missed him and how glad she was that he'd returned. He put his arms around her and gave her a squeeze, but he couldn't return her greeting because Adder had spotted him, and he couldn't look away from those big hazel eyes he'd missed so much.

"Kalil?" Adder's voice was a rough, broken whisper.

Keeping an arm around Vi to steady himself, Kalil smiled. "Hi, Adder."

Chapter Fifteen

Adder stared, dumbstruck, as Vi ran to Kalil and threw her arms around him. He had no idea what to say, or how to react. Perhaps he was seeing things.

"Kalil?" he whispered, half hoping and half fearing he'd receive an answer.

Kalil smiled. "Hi, Adder."

Adder felt as if he'd been stabbed through the heart. He'd imagined seeing Kalil here more than once, but the sound of that voice was too real to be his imagination. Kalil was actually here. It wasn't a wish this time, it wasn't a vision brought on by Adder's longing. It was truly happening.

His feet moved before he gave them permission. A heartbeat later, he stood within touching distance of Kalil. He wanted nothing more than to sweep the stubborn ass into his arms and smother him with kisses, but he managed to resist the urge. After all, he didn't yet know why Kalil was here, and he saw no point in opening himself up to emotional attack if he didn't have to.

Forcing his features into a smile, Adder held out his hand. "Hello, Kalil. It's very good to see you."

Kalil's shining eyes dimmed and his smile faded, but he took Adder's hand and shook. "Great to see you too. You look…uh. Good."

A bitter laugh bubbled up from Adder's chest before he could stop it. He looked like shit and he knew it. Months on end of restless sleep and brooding did nothing good for one's appearance. He dropped Kalil's hand. "As do you, my dear."

The corner of Kalil's mouth hitched up in silent acknowledgement of Adder's lie, and Adder felt a bit better. If they could still read each other that well, perhaps all was not lost.

"Kalil wants to come back to the band," Harpo announced, bouncing in place. "Isn't that great?"

Surprised, Adder searched Kalil's face. "Is this true?"

Kalil gnawed his bottom lip. The familiar nervous tic made something inside Adder crack and bleed. It was all he could do to keep himself from pulling Kalil close and never letting go.

"I do want to come back," Kalil answered, his voice tremulous. "If you still want me."

Adder heard both of the questions in those words, and his heart swelled. "Of course we do, darling. You've completely spoiled us for other drummers, I'll have you know."

Disappointment crumpled Kalil's face for a moment, and Adder felt like the worst sort of heel. But he couldn't promise anything more than a welcome back into the band. Not yet. Not until he'd had time to figure out where he stood with Kalil, and whether or not it was safe to open himself up after having been nearly destroyed not so long ago.

Spineless of him, of course. But he'd never been in love before. Never realized just how vulnerable he would feel when faced with someone who held the power to crush his soul with nothing but a few words. He didn't have the strength to risk himself until he felt a bit more sure.

Besides, a part of him wanted to see Kalil suffer for not only leaving, but ignoring all attempts to reconcile. Childish, perhaps. But true.

Kalil's chin lifted in a gesture of defiance Adder had seen many times before. "Well. Okay. I'm filling in for Bucket War's drummer right now, but she's supposed to be back next week so that gig's almost over. I can start practicing with y'all tomorrow, and I'm free for shows by next weekend."

Harpo whooped. "Thank fuck."

"No kidding." Vi hooked her arm through Kalil's and squeezed. "Vermillion's session drummers were pretty good, but it's like they totally didn't get our music, you know? I think you're the only one who ever has, really."

Turning his melancholy gaze from Adder, Kalil gave Vi a fond smile. "I'm glad to be back. I can't wait to start playing with y'all again."

"Can you stay for a little while today?" Adder blushed when Kalil looked at him again. *Gods, I really must control myself better than this.* "I know you have to play tonight, and I know you don't have your drum kit here, but we still have that old one in the storage room, and I'd love to get your input on a new song I've written."

Kalil stared at him with an inscrutable expression. Adder stared back, trying to keep his own expression neutral. He felt far too off balance to let anyone—least of all his secret love—see how anxious he was for Kalil to stay.

When Kalil finally spoke, his voice held a note of caution. "All right, I guess I can stay for an hour or so."

Adder couldn't stop the relieved smile which spread across his face. He knew he must look as pathetically eager as he felt. The way Kalil's eyes lit up should have calmed him, but instead it only made him more afraid.

Stop being such a sniveling baby, Adder admonished himself. *Since when have you been so scared to go after what you want? Just do it.*

Easier said than done. But Adder knew the voice in his head was right. So what if he was frightened and conflicted? He'd never backed down from a challenge in his life. Why should one from within himself rather than without be any different?

Shoving his fears to the back of his mind, Adder lifted Kalil's chin, bent and brushed a chaste kiss across his lips. Kalil's breath hitched, and Adder smiled. "Welcome back, darling."

Kalil only meant to stay an hour. He had things to do before the Bucket War show at eight, and in any case he wasn't sure he could spend too much time in Adder's company right now without having an embarrassing emotional meltdown. But the hour stretched into three and beyond before Kalil knew it. It just felt too damn good to finally be back where he belonged, even though Adder was a little cool toward him. The man's uncharacteristic caution just made Kalil more certain that he was doing the right thing, and more determined to win Adder back.

He burst through the back door at Scandalous twenty minutes before he had to be on stage. "Sorry I'm late," he said before Spike's furious glare could turn into a tirade. "Got hung up in traffic."

It was a big fat lie. Spike most likely knew that. But Kalil didn't care. He could set up his drums in five minutes flat, so it wasn't like he was holding things up.

Unsurprisingly, Spike didn't see it that way. He stalked up to Kalil with a thunderous expression. "Traffic, my ass. Where the fuck have you been?"

Kalil shrugged. If Spike wanted the truth that bad, Kalil would tell him. What the hell, right? "I went to see Adder. I'm gonna go back to drumming for him."

Shock flowed across Spike's face. Kalil grinned. He was having way too much fun with this.

"You want to be careful with that nutcase," Spike said, his voice low as if he was sharing some great secret. "I heard he's fired, like, a dozen drummers ever since Vermillion signed him."

Kalil laughed at Spike's exaggeration. "Adder's a perfectionist, that's all. We understand each other. That's why we work so well together."

Spike's eyes narrowed, and Kalil scowled. He knew that look. It was the same one he got from everyone who remembered his very public relationship with Adder and wondered how that played into his break with the band. It didn't surprise him that Spike took this long to put two and two together. His picture was probably next to "clueless" in the dictionary.

"You might want to know that he's been fucking everything on two legs ever since you left." Spike leered at him. "I'd either stay the hell away or keep lots of rubbers on hand, if I were you."

Jealousy curled in the pit of Kalil's stomach. Knowing Adder like he did, he'd figured the idiot had probably been fucking his way through Atlanta since Kalil left. Sex was Adder's chocolate ice cream—his consolation when he felt down, or angry, or conflicted.

In fact, Adder used sex to deal with practically every emotion in the book. Kalil was used to that. What he wasn't used to anymore was Adder fucking through his feelings with someone else.

He also wasn't used to being confronted with what Adder had probably been doing while they'd been apart. He knew his jealousy was irrational and unfair, but he could've cheerfully killed Spike for putting those hateful mental pictures in his head.

"Okay, well, I'm, uh...I'm gonna go put my kit together. 'Scuse me." Kalil backed away from Spike, turned and fled as fast as he could without actually running.

Thankfully, Spike did not follow him. Annie and Clark stood side by side in front of the monitors, tuning up. They both nodded to Kalil, but didn't come over to talk to him. He was glad. He had nothing against either of them, but he really wanted to be alone for a while, to think.

To daydream about Adder, you mean.

Sad, but true. Even sadder, he didn't care how pathetic he was acting. Shaking his head, he busied himself setting up his drums.

As he worked, he shoved aside useless speculation about who all Adder had fucked in the last four months and thought about his glorious afternoon with Adder, Vi and Harpo. Musically, there hadn't been any awkwardness between them. They'd fallen back into their old rhythms just as if he'd never left, and he'd felt truly happy for the first time in months. It was wonderful. He'd practically floated all the way to Scandalous when he left.

Of course if he were honest with himself, he'd admit that the main reason for the floatiness was that one fleeting kiss from Adder. So light he barely felt it, and so quick it was over before his brain could process the reality of Adder's lips on his after all this time. But his mouth still tingled from it. That single touch stirred a sharp, fierce need inside him, and he knew he'd never be able to rest until he and Adder were back together romantically as well as musically.

He laughed out loud at that. "Kalil, you're such a fucking sap."

It was true. He was a total sap, spending his time in starry-eyed daydreams of True Love.

It came as a revelation to realize he didn't care. He wanted Adder back, and he wasn't going to let anything stop him from getting his man.

Whistling "Pixie Dust" to himself, he went back to work.

The next Wednesday, Adder took Kalil to Jordan's office to put his signature to paper and officially join the Vermillion stable of musicians.

Adder was ecstatic. Kalil, however, did not quite share Adder's enthusiasm. It wasn't surprising, but it *was* disappointing, and Adder had no compunction about sharing his feelings on the matter.

"Darling, I can't believe you're still so reticent about signing this contract." He frowned at Kalil, who was sitting beside him on the sofa in Jordan's waiting room. "You've seen the revisions. They can't strand us in the midst of a tour. They've added a specific clause stating that they will finish it and get us back home, even if they decline to renew the contract in the meantime. It may not seem like much, but Jordan tells me that's unheard of for a newly signed band."

"I know, I know." Kalil chewed his thumbnail and glanced nervously at Jordan's closed office door. His right knee bounced so hard it shook the entire couch. "It's just, I've never done anything this huge before. It's fucking scary."

"Of course it is." Adder pressed a hand to Kalil's knee to hold his leg still. "It will be all right, K. I promise."

Kalil looked up to meet Adder's gaze. His dark eyes held a wariness which hadn't been there before their breakup, and it hurt Adder's heart to see it. He missed the trust they'd once had between them. One day, he hoped they would have it again.

Of course, in order to achieve that they'd both have to let go of all the leftover bad feelings between them. Adder had never actually *worked* at a relationship before. He had no idea how to go about it. But he was willing to try.

He only hoped Kalil never learned how many men and women he'd bedded in the past four months in a futile search for comfort. Something told him his dear, possessive love would not react well.

The intercom on the secretary's desk buzzed. Hugo—he of the blue hair and nimble tongue—answered it, then looked at Adder. "Guys? Jordan can see you now."

"Thank you, Hugo." Adder stood along with Kalil and took his hand. Kalil's fingers wove through his, and he felt light enough to fly.

Hugo gave Adder a coy look as they approached the desk. "I'm free tonight, Adder. Maybe I'll see you later?"

Hurt flashed swift as thought through Kalil's eyes and vanished behind a blank mask. Kalil yanked his hand away, stalked over to Jordan's office door and pulled it open. He went through without a word.

Adder stifled a groan. Of all the times for Hugo to flirt, why did it have to be now? Just because he'd taken the boy to his bed *one* time.

He glared at Hugo. "I don't think so."

The look he got in return was not friendly. "Your loss,

honey."

Adder gave him a poisonous smile. "Again, I don't think so." He hurried after Kalil while Hugo was busy spluttering in outrage.

Sinking into the chair next to the one Kalil had already claimed, Adder reached over and touched Kalil's shoulder in silent apology. He knew better than to try and hold hands again. "Hello, Jordan." He smiled at her across the desk. "Thank you for seeing us on such short notice."

"Are you kidding? I wasn't going to keep Kalil waiting." She beamed at them both. "I was just telling Kalil how thrilled Vermillion is that he's agreed to sign. Their drummers were okay—"

"They were *not.*" Adder scowled. "Competence is not enough for this band. I need genius. Therefore, Kalil is the only acceptable drummer."

Kalil hunched his shoulders. "Um. Thanks." When he glanced at Adder, his gaze was slightly warmer than it had been mere seconds ago.

Adder decided to count that as a victory.

"All right then. The drummers Vermillion provided were not satisfactory." Jordan shot an amused look at Adder before turning back to Kalil. "In any case, Kalil, we're all very happy to have you back. Do you have any further questions, or are you ready to sign?"

Adder held his breath. Jordan had spent two solid hours with Kalil the previous day, explaining the revised contract and answering questions. Adder hadn't been privy to that session, but Kalil had said later that Jordan had satisfactorily addressed all his concerns. He only hoped Kalil hadn't thought of anything in the intervening hours to keep him from putting pen to paper. Entirely aside from the desire to be with Kalil every minute of every day, Adder was rather anxious to have his drummer back.

Kalil drew a deep breath and let it out in a rush. “I’m ready to sign.”

Opening the folder on top of her desk, Jordan took out a thick sheaf of papers and slid them across to Kalil. “I’ve marked the spots you need to initial, in addition to your signature at the end.”

Adder watched as Kalil picked up the pen Jordan gave him and initialed the appropriate blanks. He hesitated for heartbeat when he reached the last page, then scribbled his name on the line. Adder got the distinct impression that the poor dear was trying to get it done before he could change his mind.

Business accomplished, Kalil set the pen down and slumped back in his chair. “Done. Now what?”

Smiling, Jordan took the signed papers and tucked them back into the folder. “Tomorrow afternoon, you join Adder, Harpo and Vi in the studio. Thank God they were able to reschedule some recording sessions after Adder fired the last drummer. Tonight, though, you need to relax a little. I’ve never seen anyone as young as you look so damn tense.”

Kalil wrinkled his nose. “I’m not tense.”

“Darling, you’re one of the most tightly wound people I’ve ever known.” Adder leaned over and pressed a lingering kiss to Kalil’s lips in order to stop the inevitable protest. “Let me take you out tonight,” he whispered, not caring that Jordan sat not three feet away, watching them. “To celebrate.”

Kalil swallowed. “Okay.”

Judging by the dazed look in Kalil’s eyes, he’d agreed to Adder’s suggestion not because of any particular interest in going out, but rather on the influence of a mutual need so strong Adder could almost smell it. Adder tangled his fingers into Kalil’s hair and wished with all his heart that they were alone.

Jordan cleared her throat, causing Kalil to jump and pull out of Adder's grip. She shook her head, but her smile was indulgent. "All right, boys. Business is concluded. You kids go out and have fun."

Adder rose and reached across the desk to squeeze Jordan's hand. "Thank you, love. Are you coming to the studio tomorrow?"

"I'll probably stop by for a while, yeah." She pressed Adder's fingers, then let go to shake hands with Kalil as he stood. "It's great to have you back, hon. See you tomorrow."

"Yeah. See you." Kalil gave Jordan a nod, then followed Adder out the door.

Ignoring Hugo's icy glare, Adder draped an arm across Kalil's shoulders as they crossed the room to the stairwell. "Where would you like to go, my dear? The city is yours tonight, and I shall be your devoted escort."

Kalil didn't look at him, and didn't speak. They descended the stairs in silence. By the time they emerged, a cold knot of dread had formed in Adder's stomach.

Taking hold of Kalil's shoulders, Adder spun him so that they were facing one another. "What's wrong, darling? Please tell me."

Kalil stared into Adder's eyes with an obvious struggle waging in his own. "Nothing. I just, I, I really don't feel like going out tonight." He dropped his gaze to the sidewalk. "Sorry."

Adder's heart plummeted into his feet, but he'd die before he let it show. Dropping his hands, he summoned the fake smile he'd relied on for months. "It's all right. Do you need a ride to your brother's house?"

Kalil laughed, though the sound was without humor. "You

don't have a car, Adder, how would you give me a ride?"

"I could pay for a cab. Or we could walk back home and I could drive you in the van."

"Oh. No, I'll take MARTA to Lenox Square and get Tony to pick me up there." Kalil met Adder's gaze again, looking torn. "I, uh. I guess I'll see you tomorrow."

"Yes." Acting on a whim, Adder took Kalil's hand, bent and kissed his knuckles. "Until then."

He turned and walked away without looking back. Gods, but Kalil was the most frustrating and inscrutable human being on the planet. Adder knew Kalil still wanted him. Why, then, did the man continue to push him away? He felt as if they were right back to where they'd started more than a year ago, only this time Adder had much more at stake than a mere flirtation.

"You wanted to know where you stood," Adder muttered to himself as he crossed the street. "I suppose you have your answer."

The thought depressed him. Even worse, however, was his own inability to change things. Never in his life had he shrunk from reaching out and taking what he wanted. It bothered him that he didn't seem capable of doing so now.

Is this what love does to a person? Does it make everyone this frightened and confused?

Lost in his thoughts, Adder turned a corner and collided with a small, curvy body. The stranger stumbled backward, cursing. "Hey, watch it."

"I'm so sorry, miss." Adder schooled his face into his most sincerely apologetic expression. "Are you quite all right?"

"Yeah, yeah." The woman brushed at her charcoal gray skirt. Her bright blue eyes fixed on Adder, and promptly heated with pure brazen lust. "Why don't you take me out for a drink?

To make up for nearly knocking me over, I mean."

Not so long ago, after Kalil left, Adder would have taken what she so clearly offered and used it to relieve his inner pain for a little while. Now, all he could think of was how close he was to getting Kalil back in his bed, and how very much he wanted that. The woman he'd just run into, though extremely attractive, was no substitute.

Her obvious interest, however, gave Adder an idea. A bold, wicked, potentially disastrous idea.

Smiling, Adder shook his head. "Tempting as that would be, I must decline. My lover is a very jealous man."

"Too bad." Hefting her purse from the ground where it had fallen, the woman gave him a nod and rakish grin. "See you around."

"I hope so." Adder bowed as the stranger walked away, her heels clicking on the concrete.

He continued on his way, strolling slowly along and thinking. The plan which had popped into his head was simple. The main difficulty lay in timing it correctly.

You're mad, Adder told himself. *Insane. If you don't execute this right, you could end up losing him for good.*

Of course, at this point, losing Kalil was a real possibility regardless. What harm could it do to force his hand? If all went as planned, he would have Kalil back in his arms within twenty-four hours. If things didn't go so well, at least he'd be no worse off than he was now.

He hoped.

Pushing his doubts to the back of his mind, he picked up his stride. He needed to get home. He had planning to do.

✧

Kalil finished his first day in the recording studio with a rolling flurry on the toms. Behind the glass, Brian leaned over and thumbed on the mic. “Done and done, kid. Great job.”

“Thanks.” Kalil set his sticks on top of the snare, stood and stretched, grinning so hard it hurt his cheeks. “Where’s everyone else? Did they leave already?” There’d been enough time left to lay down one more drum track, but not enough time for anything else. After twelve hours cooped up in this building, he could hardly blame his bandmates if they’d left already.

“Harpo and Vi are in here.” Brian jerked his thumb toward the sofa behind him.

Nodding, Kalil stepped out from behind the drum kit. He walked into the booth and plopped onto the couch between Vi and Harpo. “Wow. You know what, that’s about the longest workday I’ve ever put in, but *damn* it was fun.”

Vi laughed. “I know what you mean.”

“Don’t worry, you’ll get over that newbie excitement soon enough.” Harpo deflected the swipe Kalil aimed at his head and slapped Kalil on the back. “Me and Vi were just thinking we’d head over to Sid’s, you wanna come?”

“Yeah, sounds cool.” Kalil studied the lines on his palms. “So. Um. Where’d Adder go?”

He winced at the note of hope in his voice. *God, you’re pathetic. Still carrying the fucking torch when any moron could see he’s gone back to playing the field.*

Not that Adder wouldn’t take him back in a hot minute. Kalil knew he would. The problem was, Kalil couldn’t stand to be just one lover in Adder’s harem. Not anymore. He wanted what they’d had before, and more.

Too bad there didn’t seem to be any chance of getting it.

"He went to the break room. Said he wanted to relax for a little while." Harpo wrinkled his nose. "You know what, maybe we ought not take him to Sid's with us. He's liable to pick up the first guy or girl who smiles at him and take 'em home. And I swear to God, if it's another screamer, I'm gonna lose it."

Vi let out a gasp. "Oh my God, Harpo! You're so fucking crude."

Harpo shrugged. "No offense or anything, Special K. You were always pretty good at keeping it down."

Jesus fucking Christ. Kalil shut his eyes and reminded himself what a good friend Harpo was, and how much he'd regret it if he killed him.

While Harpo and Vi bickered about Harpo's complete lack of tact and compassion, Kalil opened his eyes and pushed to his feet. "Brian? You need us here, or can we take off?"

"Go on, I'm out of here in a few myself." Brian swiveled his chair to face them. "We'll listen to this drum track before we start the next session, but honestly I think it's a keeper."

Kalil beamed. "Cool, thanks. Well I guess we'll go on, then."

Her indignation apparently forgotten, Vi jumped up and pulled Harpo to his feet. "Thanks for everything, Brian. We'll see you Monday."

Brian waved at them as they filed out of the booth. Halfway down the hall to the lobby, Harpo stopped. "Oh damn, I almost forgot, Kalil, Adder told me to tell you to come get him before you leave."

"Me?" Kalil glanced around the empty hallway. "Why me?"

"I think he wanted to talk to you about something."

Kalil's stomach somersaulted. "Um. Okay." He stuck his hands in the back pockets of his jeans in an attempt to hide his sudden attack of nerves. "Where's the break room?"

"Down that way." Harpo pointed past the room they'd just left to where the hallway turned sharply to the right.

"Okay." Kalil started toward the bend in the corridor. An idea struck him, and he stopped and pivoted to face his friends. "You know what, why don't y'all go on ahead? Me and Adder'll meet you there whenever he's done talking."

"We can wait for you," Vi told him, at the same time as Harpo said "Okay". She glared at him. "Harpo—"

"Vi." Harpo slipped an arm around her shoulders. "You know damn well that if Adder wants to talk, it'll be a while."

"But—"

"Let's go. I'll buy you a drink." Grinning, Harpo dragged a protesting Vi toward the lobby. "See you later, K."

"Yeah, see you."

Kalil stood and watched until Vi and Harpo went through the door into the lobby. Harpo's expression screamed "I've got a secret", and Kalil wondered what in the hell he was up to.

Kalil's curiosity wasn't enough to keep him from spinning on his heel and hurrying down the hall to where Adder waited, though. He cursed himself for an idiot as he walked, his sneakers soundless on the plush carpet. He hated the way Adder could still make him feel like a schoolgirl with a stupid crush. Nearly a year as a couple ought to have cured him of that.

Of course breaking up ought to have cured him of being in love with the man, but that hadn't worked either. Which was why he'd decided to seize this unexpected time alone with Adder and tell him how he felt. Right now. Before he lost his nerve.

He turned the corner. The break room lay at the end of the short leg of the hall. Kalil took a few slow, deep breaths, then marched up to the entry, turned the knob and flung the door open.

"Adder, I need to—" Kalil stopped and stared. "Fucking hell."

Chapter Sixteen

The logical part of Kalil's brain knew he shouldn't have been so shocked to find Adder fucking some brainless twink in the studio break room. But he was. Irritatingly, the willowy boy bent over the arm of the chair with his pants around his ankles didn't seem nearly as surprised as Kalil.

Neither did Adder, as a matter of fact. Kalil had no idea what to make of *that*.

"What the fuck, Adder?" Kalil sputtered when he got his voice back.

"Be with you in a moment, darling." Adder's hips flexed, driving his cock deep into the slut-boy's ass. "A bit busy right now. You may watch if you like."

The boy moaned like the whore he clearly was, and something inside Kalil snapped.

Slamming the door behind him, Kalil crossed the room in a couple of strides, planted a hand on Adder's chest and pushed. Adder stumbled backward. The whore let out a yip when Adder's prick slid out of him.

Kalil glared at the boy. "Get out."

The slut pulled up his jeans, zipped them and headed for the door. "Bye, Adder." He shot a smirk over his shoulder as he walked out. "Good luck."

"Thank you." Pulling off the bright blue rubber—blue, good grief, where did he *get* these things?—Adder tossed it into the trashcan, leaned against the wall and smiled at Kalil. "Well, darling. What was it you needed so badly that you felt the need to interrupt?"

The bastard's sheer nerve in asking that question was aggravating. But the fact that Adder could stand there with his stupid orange shorts unzipped and his half-hard cock hanging out and not even have the grace to look embarrassed pissed Kalil the fuck off. Growling, Kalil lunged at Adder, yanked him forward by his bright yellow shirt and kissed him so hard their teeth clacked together.

He half expected Adder to push him away, considering how distant Adder had been since Kalil's return to the fold. Instead, he let out a desperate little whimper, clasped Kalil in his arms and kissed back like his life depended on it.

The second Adder's tongue wound around his, Kalil's fury shifted sideways into a need so strong his whole body shook with it. Rising on tiptoe, he hooked a leg around Adder's thigh and dug both hands into Adder's shoulders. He was about a second away from climbing Adder like a tree, but right then he didn't give a shit. After four long, lonely months, he couldn't get close enough no matter how hard he tried.

"Gods, I've missed you," Adder breathed between kisses.

"Mm. Me too." Kalil bit Adder's bottom lip, then dipped his head to suck up what he hoped would be a spectacular bruise later. "You planned this, you bastard."

"Guilty." Adder moaned, his head falling back against the wall. His hips bucked forward, and his hard prick dug into Kalil's stomach. "Uh. Fuck me."

Kalil shoved his hand between their bodies and curled his fingers around Adder's cock. They both groaned at the contact.

"Why?"

"Be...because I will *die* if I don't get your cock inside me this instant." Adder drew a deep, shuddering breath. "Gods, K, please."

Panting, Kalil twisted his hand around Adder's shaft. "No, dumbass, why'd you want me to catch you fucking that guy?"

Adder's body arched away from the wall when Kalil's thumb caught the head of his dick. "Gods! Uh. I, I wanted to...to know if... You, when you're angry, you...you don't hold back, and, and I, I wanted, I wanted..."

He trailed off, but Kalil got the point. *Oh my God. He made me jealous on purpose so I'd stake my claim on him.*

It was crazy and stupid, but strangely sweet. Something in Kalil's chest melted, and he smiled against Adder's skin. "You do realize you've turned into a one-man soap opera."

Adder let out a breathless laugh. "Or a sitcom, considering that I enlisted Harpo's assistance." His fingers wove into Kalil's hair. "Darling. Fuck me."

A fresh wave of desire rolled through Kalil's veins. God, he wanted his prick inside Adder so bad he could practically feel the heat of Adder's body already. But he had something else in mind this time.

"No," Kalil murmured into the curve of Adder's neck. "I want *you* to fuck *me* this time." He lifted his head and stopped Adder's standard *I don't top* line with a stern look. "You just had your dick up that little slut's ass, so don't even say it. Just fuck me."

Adder's face flushed red. His gaze dropped. Without a word, he fished another condom out of his shorts pocket. Snatching the packet from him, Kalil ripped it open and rolled the rubber onto Adder's erection.

"Green. Nice." Kalil shook his head with a smile. He'd missed Adder's weird penchant for colored condoms. It reminded him of their early days together. He lifted his arms. "Get my pants down."

This time, Adder's gaze met Kalil's and locked on. Staring straight into Kalil's eyes, Adder undid Kalil's jeans with shaking fingers and shoved them down. Kalil hissed when his prick caught on the edge of his underwear on the way down.

Adder smoothed his thumb over the tip of Kalil's cock, then had to snake an arm around his waist to keep him from collapsing to the floor when his legs decided to stop holding him up. "Sorry."

"'S okay." Shoving Adder's hand away with a huge effort, Kalil turned and bent over the arm of the chair. Adder whimpered, and Kalil grinned. "You better have lube."

From behind him, Kalil heard the sound of a K-Y packet being torn open. "Darling, have you ever known me to be without emergency lube?"

Adder sounded far more composed than he had a few seconds ago. Kalil didn't like that. He wanted Adder open, raw, completely without control. Before he could do anything about it, though, two long, slick fingers penetrated him, and he couldn't be bothered to think that hard anymore.

A violent shudder shook him head to toe when Adder found and massaged his prostate. "God. Fuck. C'mon."

The fingers pulled out of him. He felt his cheeks spread, then the blunt head of Adder's prick nudged his hole. A push, a brief burn, and Adder was inside him for the first time. That he actually remembered, anyway. It felt incredible. He wished he could bottle the sensation and keep it.

"Oh, gods." Adder's chest pressed to Kalil's back, his hair falling forward to tickle Kalil's ear. He planted one hand on the chair beside Kalil's. The other slipped between Kalil's legs to grasp his cock. "So tight."

That's what happens when you don't get fucked for over a year. Kalil kept the thought to himself. Not that he would've been able to string together such a coherent sentence at this point.

Arching his back, he rubbed his cheek against Adder's and pressed backward so that Adder's prick pushed balls-deep into him.

Adder cried out. His cock pulsed and swelled in Kalil's ass. "Can't… I can't…" He buried his face in Kalil's hair. "Not going to last."

Kalil didn't care if neither of them made it through more than a few thrusts. They'd have time for leisurely lovemaking later. Right now, he just wanted Adder to pound him flat.

"Move," he ordered, rocking his hips to illustrate his point. "Fuck me."

To his immense relief, Adder did as he was told. He hammered Kalil's ass in short, hard strokes. His hand on Kalil's shaft didn't move, but Kalil didn't care. Every time Adder thrust into him, the movement caused his cock to rub against the arm of the chair. After such a long time with nothing but his own touch, this was more than enough to get him off.

Sure enough, a whole minute hadn't passed before Adder groaned and went still, his prick buried deep in Kalil's butt. Tremors shook his body. His hand clenched tight around Kalil's cock, and Kalil went off like a rocket, pumping what felt like gallons of come all over the chair. He managed to keep his usual banshee wail down to a soft keening. The last thing he wanted was for some unsuspecting intern or secretary or security guard to hear him and decide they needed to see what all the noise was. Not that there was probably anyone much around at nearly midnight, but you never could tell. Recording studios tended to be busy at weird times.

"Mmmmmm." Adder sighed and nuzzled Kalil's ear. "Magnificent, darling. Simply magnificent."

"I'd say." Kalil twisted his head enough to kiss the corner of Adder's mouth. "Better get up. Someone else is eventually gonna walk in here, and I'd rather not be bent over with your cock up my ass when they do."

Adder laughed. The movement dislodged his shrinking cock from Kalil's hole. Kalil yelped, and Adder laughed harder. The sound was one of pure joy, and it was infectious. Chuckling, Kalil nudged Adder with one elbow. "Up. You're heavy after you come."

"Very well." Adder peeled himself off Kalil's back, hauled Kalil to a standing position and kissed his shoulder. "Oh my. Look what a mess you've made, darling."

Kalil looked, and winced. "Damn. I better clean that up before it dries."

"In a moment." Spinning Kalil around, Adder took off his shirt and used it to wipe the semen from Kalil's groin and thighs. He pulled up and fastened Kalil's jeans. He'd already removed the rubber and done up his shorts, Kalil noticed. "Kiss me, my beautiful Kalil."

God, it had been so fucking long since Kalil had heard Adder call him that. His throat closed up. Winding both arms around Adder's waist, Kalil lifted his face for Adder's kiss. It was sweet and soft this time, and that was every bit as good as the hungry, near-brutal one from before.

When they drew apart, Adder rested his forehead against Kalil's with a contented hum. "I suppose we should clean up our mess now."

"In a second." Kalil cupped Adder's face in his hands and

peered into his eyes. "You've always said you don't top. After that first time, you sure as hell never topped me. So why were you topping when I walked in on you and that fucking whore?"

"A friend and former lover, darling. Not a whore."

"Whatever. Just answer the question, okay?"

"I tried to let other men fuck me after you left. But I couldn't." Adder fell silent for a moment, his gaze searching Kalil's. "I can't stand for anyone but you to be inside me anymore."

In spite of the automatic surge of jealousy at the mention of Adder having sex with anyone but him, Kalil knew Adder well enough to know exactly what that meant. The knowledge burned away the lingering remains of his loneliness and set up a warm glow deep in his belly.

Framing Adder's face between his hands, Kalil smiled. "I love you too."

Epilogue

"Oh, oh fuck yeah!" Kalil's fingers tightened in Adder's hair as he came. "God. Uh."

Pressing Kalil's hips against the wall with both hands to hold him still, Adder swallowed the warm, slick come as it pulsed from Kalil's cock. Even after Kalil's orgasm wound to a halt, Adder held his softening prick in his mouth, giving it a lick now and then.

Sucking each other off before a show had become rather a ritual for them since getting back together almost eight months ago. They'd tried fucking, but Adder found it terribly distracting when semen trickled from his hole onstage, so they'd gone back to using oral pleasure for pre-performance relaxation.

Adder had no problem with that. He adored the feel of his love's erection in his mouth, the taste of Kalil's come, his sharp male scent. This new tradition was one Adder hoped to continue for as long as they were able to totter onstage.

When the sound of applause and whistles drifted from the direction of the stage, Kalil tugged Adder's head back by the hair. Adder reluctantly let Kalil's cock pop free of his lips. He gazed up at his lover with a wide smile. "Darling, we still have plenty of time. We don't go on for half an hour. And since we now have an actual road crew, that time is our own."

Kalil's nose wrinkled, and Adder couldn't help laughing.

Jordan had somehow talked Kalil into letting the roadies set up and tune his drums for him when they began their tour almost six weeks ago. Kalil had stopped worrying out loud by now, but Adder privately thought the dear man wished he could take over again.

Really, though, setting up their own instruments was no longer an option. *Raven,* their first album with Vermillion Records, was such a huge hit they often couldn't go out in public without being surrounded by young men and women wanting an autograph, or simply to touch or speak to them. Appearing on stage prior to the start of the show would have started a riot among the fans.

"Yeah, well. I can at least watch from the sidelines and make sure they do it right." Kalil tucked his privates back into his pants and zipped up while Adder climbed to his feet. "Don't you ever worry that they're gonna tune your violin wrong or something?"

"Sweetheart, you know I take care of my violin myself before I ever allow the roadies to touch it." Adder took Kalil's hand in his. "The most they have to do is make minor adjustments."

Kalil shook his head as the two of them left the dressing room together. "Harpo does the same thing with his bass. But both of y'all make fun of me all the time for wanting to do my drums myself."

"We're not making fun, my love. Merely teasing."

"Po-ta-to, po-tah-to."

Smiling, Adder lifted Kalil's hand and kissed it. "It's much easier for the two of us to tune up backstage. Drums are different."

"Damn straight."

They stopped in the wings to the side of the stage. Harpo

and Vi were already there, talking with the opening band, Backdoor Quickie. The group had been hired to open for Adder for the entire five-month tour, and the two bands had hit it off right from the start. BQ's odd but compelling mix of bluegrass and speed punk was quite popular with Adder's fans. Adder saw a bright future ahead for the three young women.

After a few minutes BQ left to change clothes. Adder and his friends huddled together, talking quietly while they watched the road crew take down Backdoor Quickie's set and put together theirs.

The time passed swiftly, as it always did. It seemed only a few minutes had passed before the crew leader sauntered backstage and nodded to Adder. "Y'all are set."

The four of them grinned at each other. Adder felt his bandmates' excitement as keenly as his own, and it buoyed his spirit like nothing else. "It's time, my loves. Ready?"

"Hell yeah." Harpo adjusted the red felt Fedora atop his head. "Vi? After you, milady."

Laughing, Vi kissed each of them on the cheek. "Let's kill 'em, guys."

She glided out into the glare of the spotlight, her lavender dress flowing around her ankles, and the crowd erupted. Harpo followed, hands held out before him as if to catch the audience's adoration like raindrops in his cupped palms.

Adder and Kalil looked at each other. Kalil's dark eyes shone with a bliss that Adder knew stemmed not so much from a fondness for performing as from the happiness they'd found with each other.

"I love you," Adder said, letting his heart show in his face. "So very much."

He declared his feelings prior to every show—another tradition—but familiarity with the words hadn't dimmed the light which shone in Kalil's eyes each time. Reaching up to cup Adder's cheek in his palm, Kalil rose on tiptoe and kissed him. "I love you too. Now let's do this, yeah?"

"Yes, indeed."

Hands still linked, they walked out on stage. Screams and wild applause greeted them, and Adder laughed out loud for sheer joy.

Sweeping Kalil into his arms, Adder claimed a deep, possessive kiss before letting him go. Kalil smacked Adder's backside and waved at the audience before taking his place at the drums. The crowd loved it, of course. They always did. Adder and Kalil's romance was nearly as popular as their music.

Walking over to the stand holding his violin, Adder picked up the instrument and went back to the mic. "Good evening, my dears. My name is Adder, and we are here for your pleasure."

The audience cheered with one voice, and Adder's heart swelled with the sound. It seemed more beautiful than ever now that the rest of his existence was no longer empty. He hadn't known it was empty before he found his love. But he recognized it now, and was grateful every day for the man who made his life complete.

The man who was currently waiting, along with Vi and Harpo, for Adder to start the show.

Tucking his violin beneath his chin, Adder touched the bow to the strings and began to play.

About the Author

Ally Blue is acknowledged by the world at large (or at least by her heroes, who tend to suffer a lot) as the Popess of Gay Angst. She has a great big penis hat and rides in a bullet-proof Plexiglas bubble in Christmas parades. Her harem of manwhores does double duty as bodyguards and as sinspirational entertainment. Her favorite band is Radiohead, her favorite color is lime green and her favorite way to waste a perfectly good Saturday is to watch all three extended version LOTR movies in a row. Her ultimate dream is to one day ditch the evil day job and support the family on manlove alone. She is not a hippie or a brain surgeon, no matter what her kids' friends say.

To learn more about Ally Blue, please visit www.allyblue.com. Send an email to Ally at ally@allyblue.com or join her Yahoo! group to join in the fun with other readers as well as Ally! http://groups.yahoo.com/group/loveisblue/

My Bookstore & More
www.mybookstoreandmore.com
Green for the planet.
Great for your wallet.

Lightning Source UK Ltd.
Milton Keynes UK
03 June 2010

155035UK00001B/170/P